Hawking

Danger Bluff, Book Two

Becca Jameson

Pepper North

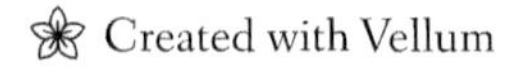
Created with Vellum

About the Book

Welcome to Danger Bluff where a mysterious billionaire brings together a hand-selected team of men at an abandoned resort in New Zealand. They each owe him a marker. And they all have something in common–a dominant shared code to nurture and protect. They will repay their debts one by one, finding love along the way.

Hawking

A mysterious billionaire saved my life.

Now, I owe him.

My team's job: Save Celeste no matter what it takes.

My goal: Convince her she's mine.

Celeste

I was so close to finding the cure.

Why was I suddenly fired?

Danger Bluff will be the perfect place to hide.

If only that ripped, former military guy didn't ooze Daddy vibes.

Prologue

"Unfortunately, your mother isn't responding to any conventional treatments. The cancer progressed too far before it was detected."

"So, what are you telling me?" Hawking stared at the doctor standing in front of him. He shut out all the machinery and people bustling around them to focus on the specialist's solemn face.

"She has six months, maybe eight."

"There's nothing you can do for her? You said conventional treatments. What about unconventional ones?"

The doctor hesitated and then spoke, "We're seeing a new medication extend the life of terminal cancer patients. Most importantly, it improves their quality of life," Dr. Ramirez said.

"Then put her on that medication," Hawking demanded.

"It's not covered by insurance and is very expensive. Unaffordable for most."

"I don't care. Whatever it is. Start her on that," Hawking repeated.

"I can't do that until the medicine is ordered, and it must be paid for in advance," the doctor shared quietly. His voice was markedly different from the former military man's commands.

Hawking took a deep breath and reminded himself this wasn't a military operation. The only order that would make an impact here was a money order. He exhaled and asked in a softer voice, "How much do I need to get, and who do I pay?"

"The last total I heard was a million dollars for a ninety-day supply. I'll have the billing department contact you today with the exact amount and the details if you feel that might be possible. In the meantime, I'd also like you to approve of having hospice come in to make your mother comfortable. Then they will already be in place."

"That's end-of-life care, right?"

"Yes. The procedure will involve an end-of-lifesaving treatment. They focus on pain control and support of a patient's quality of life."

"Without it, would you continue treatment?" Hawking asked, hoping that his questions were the right ones.

"No. She is not responding to the treatment. There is no value in continuing it."

"I want her as comfortable as possible."

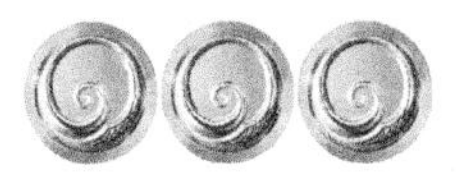

How can I get a million dollars?

Hawking sat by his mother's side in the hospital. She'd escaped from the pain into sleep. Soon, she'd leave to go stay with his sister. The last thing Agatha Winther wanted was to stay here.

He thought of a half-dozen ways to get that kind of

money and threw them away as impossible. Robbing a bank, printing his own money, even selling everything he owned wouldn't work.

A flash of all the military-grade weapons piled up in the warehouse of the arms manufacturer Hawking worked for popped into his head. A huge shipment was going out tomorrow. If he could arrange a deal for someone to intercept the arms as it was moved, he could raise what he needed. Just selling the information on the route would do it. Illegal dealers would pay top dollar to get their hands on those guns.

He pushed away the thought of how this caliber of weaponry would damage the world. This was his mother.

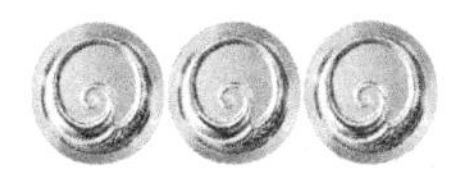

"I'm afraid I've changed the terms of our agreement."

Hawking stared at the scarred, ex-military man in front of him and felt the enormous lump of dread in his stomach double. He'd done all he could to help with the recovery of the guns from the bad guys staring at him with knowing smirks. The hidden trackers he'd placed inside each shipping container and the automated message that would be sent to the authorities within thirty minutes would almost ensure they could recover the weapons.

"Look, man, I don't know what you're thinking, but you can't go back on our deal," Hawking said, trying to bluff. He had no intention of ever repeating this again. "You'll lose a resource for future sales."

"You'll get me weapons whenever I need them."

"Why would I do that if you're not paying?" Hawking scoffed, trying to keep his don't-fuck-with-me attitude in full view.

"I have a picture of you in this exchange. You don't want those shown to your boss, the government, or the cops."

"That would shut you down as well," Hawking pointed out and saw the man's face harden. *Score one point for me.*

"Then we could just kill you. You're not the only source for weapons in this town or for this company. We'll take these while you decide whether you'd like to die here or live to make another delivery."

"I can't let you do that," Hawking announced, drawing his weapon and shifting toward an immense crane on the dock.

The glow of a red target light on his chest motivated him to dive to safety behind the large piece of machinery. Shots filled the air. The automatic blasts clued him in that he was horribly out-gunned, and his chances were slim to survive this.

He peeked around the large tire he hid behind and saw a shadow approaching from behind the men, firing before he had time to jerk his head back. *Good guys or bad guys?* Hawking shook his head. It didn't matter. Either way, he was screwed.

After a flurry of gunfire, a male voice called, "Hawking Winther, you can take these back to your company now."

They knew his name? "What? Who are you?" Hawking looked around the crane to see bodies scattered across the area and six men standing in a semi-circle around his position.

"Come on out."

Shaking his head, Hawking took a chance and stepped away from his cover. While his hands were up, he held his gun ready.

"Your mom's treatment is funded. You have other things to do besides go to jail or get killed here." The man walked forward and handed him a round token. "This is a marker. We'll need your experience in the future."

The men turned to go, leaving Hawking gawking after them as they merged into the shadows. He shouted after them, "I don't get it. You've saved me and my mom, and I just owe you a favor?"

"You'll owe more than that," the voice responded from a distance.

Chapter One

"What do you mean my research is flawed?" Celeste stared at the man sitting behind the large desk. She'd never liked the self-inflated supervisor who forced everyone to call him by his PhD title and last name in the casual lab atmosphere.

"It's common practice to review a sample of the documentation for testing, Celeste. Yours was randomly selected and failed," Dr. Hughes stated. "The computer review reported concerns, so another scientist examined it. I don't know what your purpose was in introducing false data, but your research is now canceled, and you are terminated."

"Canceled?" Celeste could only repeat the word that stood out to her in all the madness her boss spouted. "But Dr. Hughes, I'm on the edge of some very exciting breakthroughs that will allow us to stop cancer cells from multiplying quickly."

"You can drop the act, Celeste. Your research is a flop, and you're fired." He pressed a button, and a large man stepped into the office. "This man will escort you to the lab for you to retrieve your personal effects and then off the grounds. You are not to return. I would not suggest that you use our firm as a reference here in New Zealand or anywhere."

"Dr. Hughes! I've worked here for almost eight years. My research is not flawed. It needs to continue. I'm close to finding a viable way to stop cancer from spreading."

"Good luck in the future, Celeste." The administrator looked down at the papers in front of him and ignored her as Celeste stood in front of him.

Pissed beyond thinking straight, she pounded a fist on his desk. "You know there's nothing wrong with my research. What's going on here?"

"Thomas? Please deal with this." Dr. Hughes did not look up as the security guard Celeste said good morning to every day when she arrived took her arm and towed her away from the desk and through the door.

"We can do this the hard way, or you can preserve your dignity," the guard told her after closing the executive's door.

"I'll go get my things," Celeste said, stiffening her spine.

She walked back to her lab and found her computer gone. Thank goodness she'd saved her work before reporting to the meeting. Doubly saved it, that is. Shrugging off her company lab coat, she grabbed her large purse from under the desk and set it in the chair. Celeste opened the middle drawer and gathered the few things she'd stored inside: Chapstick, hand lotion, pen, blue-tooth external hard drive.

"Wait. You can't take that."

Celeste's heart thudded inside her chest as she tried to look cool. Her fingers clamped on the outer housing of the drive as he reached forward.

"That belongs to the company," he said sternly as he plucked the company pen from her hand.

When her heart stopped fluttering drastically in her

chest, Celeste put the small tech box along with the other things he'd deemed harmless into her tote. The last thing she selected to take was the cute, black cat figurine from the top of her desk. "That's everything."

The security guard opened the other drawers and found nothing. "You don't have any company property in that big purse, do you?"

"I have my phone, wallet, and an emergency pack of tampons. You're welcome to check," she said, waving a hand at the bag.

Just as she thought, the mere mention of feminine products made the man back off. She picked up her purse and looped it over her shoulder. Avoiding the curious looks of the other scientists as she followed Thomas out of the lab area, Celeste walked through the doors and didn't hesitate. She kept placing one foot in front of the other until she reached a park three blocks away.

Heading for a spot where she frequently ate lunch, Celeste ducked behind a hedge to a bench very few people seemed to know existed. She collapsed and dropped her face into her hands. *What just happened?*

An hour later, she forced herself to catch the bus back to her apartment. She'd certainly heard of random reviews of research. Those usually took weeks, and the head scientist was involved to answer questions and explain what hypotheses they'd tested, refined, and/or abandoned. Never in her experience was a review conducted with the sole purpose of firing a scientist.

There had been baffling theories in the past. Some of the scientists involved had made the most remarkable discoveries. Thinking outside the box was rewarded. It led to breakthroughs, like hers. She was only baby steps away from a major discovery in cancer research. Everything had lined up perfectly. What did they think they'd found that was wrong?

Celeste dragged herself upstairs and automatically changed into her running clothes. She always ran after work. It helped her synthesize everything she'd done throughout the day. The ideas she came up with as she powered through a few miles were the direct result of giving her mind a task and letting it work as she worked out.

The only thing that developed on this run was a determination to prove they were wrong. Back in her apartment, she showered and pulled on her favorite pajamas before diving into the data. Nothing. There was nothing wrong. Her calculations were perfect.

Unable to stop herself, Celeste grabbed her personal computer and tried logging into the system to find the negative documentation that had to be in her file. Her login and password didn't function. They'd very efficiently removed her access.

Celeste typed a different login into the computer and let it fill in the password for her. She'd dated a guy in the personnel department a month ago. He'd logged into her laptop in an emergency, and her system had saved his access.

Zipping through the files, she accessed hers and found the newest file labeled "Termination Proof." She downloaded it quickly and logged out of the system. Determined, she compared her research to the file. There. That wasn't right. Someone had altered the results of one of her tests. No wonder they didn't think her research was valid. She would have questioned it as well if that had been the correct data.

Sure that there had been a problem, she copied the screenshots of the discrepancy and emailed them to Dr. Hughes. Feeling better than she had all day, Celeste decided to run to the all-night diner and celebrate with pancakes—her favorite splurge meal. Thinking she might want to look at the data saved on it again, Celeste added her laptop to her large purse. She applauded the day she'd decided the oversized handbag would be a more stylish way to carry everything.

Changing quickly into jeans, she looked at her childhood stuffie on the bed. Hades, the black cat, should come along for the celebration. She could fit, too. No one would see her in Celeste's big bag.

A few hours later, stuffed with pancakes, Celeste rode the elevator up to her floor. When it opened, she could see her door. Something looked wrong. Quietly, she tiptoed closer to the door and stopped. The bottom edge of the door had a red square by the hinge.

Heart pounding, she dashed back to the elevator and frantically stabbed the button. The doors reopened immediately, and she quickly entered and jabbed the ground floor. Her mechanical engineer roommate in college had designed the red-square trick to show when someone had been in their room. It was a simple device that activated only when her phone wasn't nearby and the room door was opened.

Quickly, she called the police and reported a break-in. The dispatcher instructed her to go into the bathroom in the apartment building lobby and lock the door. Listening to every creak and sound as she hid in the corner of the room, Celeste stayed on the phone until an officer knocked on the door and identified himself.

"Someone ransacked your apartment. It appears they were looking for something," the officer said, studying her reaction closely.

Celeste sucked in a breath. Was there any chance someone from her company would come after her? "I'm a research scientist who spends three-fourths of her life in the lab."

"Working on anything someone would be interested in?"

"A cure for cancer."

"That could make someone a lot of money," the officer replied, raising his eyebrows.

"Yes, but this isn't the movies. People don't come after scientists. They don't even know we exist," Celeste muttered.

"I would suggest you find somewhere to stay for a while. Then, change the locks or consider moving. I'll gladly escort you to your apartment and wait while you pack a few things to take with you."

"Thanks. I'll do that," she said gratefully, pushing her hair back from her face with a shaky hand.

Walking into her apartment, Celeste looked at the disaster that had happened while she'd been eating pancakes. What if she had been at home? She quickly gathered running gear, several pairs of jeans and tops, and a bunch of underwear from the piles tossed all over her bedroom. The intruder had broken her e-reader and had left her vibrator buzzing on her bed.

Embarrassed, she turned the thing off and dumped it in the trashcan. That would never touch her again. The cop's expression didn't change. He just stood in the doorway, monitoring her and the apartment.

Rolling her suitcase over the ton of things tossed to the floor, Celeste picked up her bag, catching sight of Hades. Thank goodness she'd taken her stuffie. They could have torn her apart. Not letting herself think about that horrific thought, she forced herself to think. What else did she need?

Celeste dashed into the bathroom. She grabbed a cosmetic bag and filled it with the small amount of makeup she owned—basically lip gloss and mascara—and the birth control pills she used to control her heavy periods. Finalizing her packing, she added a handful of emergency tampons and over-the-counter pain relievers.

Making one last stop in her kitchen, Celeste scooped up her black cat cookie jar in the crook of her arm. When she rejoined the police officer, she thanked him for staying with her as she gathered her things.

"Just doing my job, miss. Is your car close?"

"I'll call a rideshare to take me to my sister's."

"Stay in the lighted lobby and triple-check the license plate. Call if you have any concerns," he recommended, looking worried as he handed her a card with his name and contact information.

In a few minutes, her door was closed and locked as securely as possible until the apartment manager could make repairs. She rode down in the elevator with the police officer and pulled out her phone to order transportation as soon as she reached the lobby.

She didn't have any siblings, and her parents had both passed, but she hadn't wanted the officer to think she had nowhere to go. She did have friends here in New Zealand. Not close ones, but a few she kept in touch with sporadically. Molly Smith was the closest friend, but Celeste wouldn't call her either. She didn't want to endanger her.

Searching her brain and her phone, she came up with two hotels next door to each other. Plugging one address into the rideshare app, she waited for the designated car to arrive. Looking in every direction, she walked out far enough to see the license plate. As soon as she verified the car and driver, she stowed her things in the backseat beside her, and the driver pulled into traffic.

Nervous now, Celeste watched behind her and noticed a car pulling out from a nearby parking spot. After two turns, she was convinced it was following her. As they drove under the streetlights, she memorized the make and color of the car and even got the first two letters on the license plate. Quickly, she turned off her phone.

When they arrived at her destination, Celeste darted into the hotel, acting like she knew what she was doing, and immediately turned down the hallway leading to the side exit. Her heart thudded inside her chest as she dashed across the darkened gap between the two buildings.

Thank goodness the other hotel's side door was open. She headed to the front desk to book a room overlooking the front entrance. They didn't want to allow her to check in without a credit card or identification. Celeste explained about the break-in and invented the robbery of her wallet. She flashed the police officer's card as proof while offering cash and a cash deposit.

As soon as she let herself into the darkened hotel room, Celeste set her things beside the door and locked it securely. She carefully made her way through the room lit only by the light coming from the cracked bathroom door, then peeked out the window and spotted the same car that had been following her parked below on the street. Quickly, she closed the curtains before turning on the light in the bathroom. Sliding down the wall, she wrapped her arms around her knees and curled into a ball, trying to stop herself from shaking.

What the hell was happening? Twenty-four hours ago, her life had been monotonous and boring. Now, her supervisor had fired her and accused Celeste of falsifying, or at least bungling, data. Then someone had broken into her apartment and now followed her. She needed to put some distance between herself and the lab. They were the only people who could be involved.

Feeling shattered, Celeste crawled toward her belongings, drew the cookie jar toward her, and leaned against the wall for support. She took the top off and dropped the dozen cookies into the trash before pulling out the plastic bag concealed at the bottom with a deep sigh of relief. Thanking her mother's distrust of banks that had resulted in Celeste always wanting to have cash on hand, she would have money to live on for a while.

After forcing herself to her feet, she showered and rescued Hades from her bag. Then, leaving the light on in the bathroom, she got into bed and crashed into sleep. Her mind escaped from reality, unable to process anything else.

Chapter Two

"Breaktime's over," Magnus announced, pushing himself to his feet and walking away from the gathered group to collapse into the gaming chair in front of the computers.

Hawking followed him and held his hand out to drop the flash drive into his teammate's palm. He held his breath as Magnus plugged it into the port. Everyone stood from the table and joined them.

A whirl of the system and several keystrokes later, a picture of a slim woman with eye protection over her glasses popped onto the screen. Hawking immediately noted that her plump lips seemed even more sexy when compared to her no-fuss appearance. A full body shot with her wrapped in a white lab coat, concealing her shape, filled another screen. A final picture was displayed, and all the men, including Rocco, took a deep inhale.

"Hey!" Sadie protested, whacking her Daddy's arm.

"Sorry, Little girl. I was not expecting that from the first two pictures," Rocco apologized as he pulled her close to his body, turning away from that last photo.

A low whistle pierced the air, and Hawking turned to glare at Phoenix. The buff man lifted his hands immediately and warded off the larger man's attention. "I'm just human, dude."

Hawking studied the picture that had startled everyone. The woman wore a sequined green gown that perfectly matched her enormous eyes, unmasked by sturdy glasses. The material revealed a slim but curvaceous figure he hadn't expected lurking under her lab coat. Exquisitely made up, the woman could have been a movie star.

"You have to admit, Hawking, she's supremely hot," Caesar said. When Hawking leveled a glare of infinite magnitude his way, the large man added, "We're Daddies, looking for our Littles, but we're not dead."

"You will be," Hawking growled, surprising himself with the level of protectiveness he felt before even meeting her.

"Don't you think we should hear what Magnus has to tell us about her?" Sadie chimed in, clearly trying to hide her amusement but failing.

Hawking glanced at the only person in the room who apparently had a voice of reason this evening. Sadie Miller was also the only woman in the room. She was not only the reception manager for Danger Bluff Mountain Resort, but she was Rocco's Little girl.

Magnus grunted his agreement. "This is Celeste Blanke," he said, reading from the data displayed on the screen. "She's a research scientist specializing in cancer treatment and cures. The company where she has worked for seven years fired her last week with the allegation of doctoring her findings. Previous phone records to friends reveal Celeste believes she's close to determining a compound that would keep cancer cells from multiplying."

Hawking walked forward to stare at the young woman

wearing the protective laboratory gear. Could she create something that could prevent other mothers from suffering? "Is her company correct? Is her research bogus?" he asked.

"According to phone records, Celeste hasn't contacted anyone since being let go from the research firm. She sent one message to her supervisor when she returned home that contained screenshots she felt disproved the allegation of bad data. Her phone hasn't been used since calling the police to report a break-in at her apartment that evening and to call a rideshare to a hotel that reports she did not check in. The device was turned off after she was dropped off and has not been turned back on. She booked a reservation here under a friend's name without providing a departure date," Magnus added.

"How do you know her friend isn't coming on a vacation?"

"Unless her buddy is leaving a husband with five kids under eight and three large dogs to fend for themselves for an undetermined amount of time, it's Celeste. Also, facial recognition has her on the ferry coming from the north to the south island. She arrives tomorrow," Magnus said after combing through the information.

"She's from New Zealand?" Hawking asked.

"A Kiwi born and bred," Magnum answered.

"Does the report imply that we should expect trouble?" Phoenix asked.

"She's arriving under an assumed name. Her apartment was ransacked, and she didn't choose to stay at the hotel where she'd had the rideshare drop her off. She's not using her phone and has made her first mistake by using a known associate's name. If the last hours before she disappeared off the grid are any indication, yes," Magnus shared, making Hawking's stomach drop.

"Since when does a scientist's experiments to solve cancer make her the target for what seems like a very sophisticated attack?" Rocco questioned.

"She has to be so scared," Sadie whispered, tucking herself close to Rocco and settling happily on his lap when Rocco plucked Sadie from her chair.

"You are to say nothing to Celeste when she checks in if you're at the desk, Little girl," Rocco decreed. "Hawking, where is the safest place for her room?"

"Put her on the fourth floor, away from the emergency stairs and near the elevator," Hawking said.

Sadie nodded and made a note in her phone before asking Hawking, "Do you want me to forward any reservations she makes for activities to you?"

"No," Hawking said. "Magnus is going to figure out how to use her keycard as a location device. Then, we should know where she is throughout her stay." He glanced at Magnus after making the challenge.

"On it. I should be able to lock on her keycard. Sadie, will you do me a favor and choose a room for Celeste first thing in the morning?" Magnus asked.

"Of course. Do you want me to bring it to you when the keycard is matched to the room?" Sadie asked.

"If you could. I'll bring it back to you by mid-morning so you can give it to her when she checks in," Magnus told her.

"Magnus, I want that signal to show up on my phone," Hawking stated.

"As head of security, right?" Caesar teased.

"Absolutely," Hawking confirmed.

"Right." Phoenix dragged out the word to imply doubt.

After almost setting Phoenix on fire with a pointed glare, Hawking turned to Magnus. "Let me read all the information on the drive."

"Of course. Sit at that monitor," he said, pointing, "and I'll forward everything there. You can make copies of anything you need to remember and forward them to your mailbox here at Danger Bluff. However, I wouldn't send anything through any other servers."

Hawking nodded and sat before the computer to read and take careful notes on his phone. His big fingers made the process slow and arduous. When Sadie appeared at his elbow with a pad of paper and a pen, he nodded his thanks. She simply patted him on the shoulder and returned to sit next to her Daddy.

Rocco scooped her feet up into his lap and slipped off her sensible heels to massage her feet. She moaned in pleasure as he soothed her overworked muscles from filling in everywhere. The resort had only been open a week, so everyone was still exhausted at the end of each day.

Hawking wasn't the only one on edge. They'd all been vigilant as guests had begun arriving.

Hawking knew the idea that Celeste could be his Little, just as Sadie had turned out to be Rocco's, was farfetched. There was no way the mysterious Baldwin Kingsley could know that the scientist would be his match. Rocco and Sadie had just been a lucky coincidence.

"Do you think she's your Little?" Sadie asked, interrupting his thoughts.

"It's your bedtime, Little girl," Rocco interjected, saving Hawking from trying to answer that question. Rocco winked at Hawking as he led Sadie to the elevator.

As the elevator door closed, Hawking heard Sadie ask, "He *is* her Daddy, isn't he? I could tell from the look on his face."

"We'll see..."

The rest of Rocco's answer was cut off as the elevator

doors closed and the car rose to their suites on the top floor. It surprised Hawking to discover he wanted to know what his teammate thought as well. Tomorrow and her arrival would be here soon. Hawking would have to wait to find out for himself.

Chapter Three

As Hawking was talking to the security guard at the side gate, a car pulled up. The driver rolled down the window to ask, "Is this the rideshare drop-off?"

The security guard sighed as he glanced at Hawking. "Sorry, Boss. Their system must be telling the drivers the wrong place. This is the third driver to stop here."

"Good thing I stopped by to check on how things are going. I'll take care of this."

Hawking pulled a business card out of his pocket as he walked forward to greet the driver. "Looks like the directions are off. Could you send a message to the company with this update? I can help your passenger from here."

"Will do. Thanks!" The driver popped out of his car and pulled a small suitcase from the back. The passenger traveled light.

"I'd rather go to the front door, please," the woman called nervously as she stepped out of the vehicle to keep an eye on her bag.

Hawking recognized her immediately. Carefully, he controlled his expression so he wouldn't reveal that he knew who she was. Celeste Blanke.

"Hi, I'm Hawking Winther. I'm the head of security. Welcome to Danger Bluff. How about if I take you to registration and give you a scenic tour on the way?" he asked. He deliberately stood so she could see his polo shirt with the resort logo, along with his name and title.

"I guess that would be okay," the woman answered.

In a flash, the driver was gone.

Hawking took the handle of her suitcase to roll it over to the Jeep he used to drive around the property. "May I take your tote?" he asked, holding out a hand for the oversized bag she kept balanced on her shoulder.

"No, thank you. I'll hold on to my purse."

After easily hefting her suitcase into the back of the vehicle, he escorted her to the passenger side and opened the door. As he watched, she lifted the heavy bag onto the floor and then scrambled up into the cab. When she lost her balance, she fell backward, colliding with him. He stabilized her by wrapping his hands around her slender waist and giving her a boost.

"Sorry, I guess I'm tired," she murmured.

"I love this vehicle. It goes almost everywhere, but it is high to get into," he said before jogging around the front of the jeep and climbing into the driver's side.

Starting the engine, he waved to the security guard and promised, "I'll make a call when I get back to my office about the drop-off point."

"Thanks, boss."

"It'll take five minutes to get there," he assured the woman sitting stiffly in her chair. "I'd ask if this was your first time to the resort, but since we just reopened, that's pretty obvious. May I ask your name?"

"I'm Ce... I'm Molly Smith."

"Hi, Molly. I think you're going to love it here. Over on the bluff, you can dare to try rock climbing. There's snorkeling and scuba diving in the water. Hiking, swimming—even helicopter tours. Pretty much anything you could want to do on vacation," he informed her after ignoring her bobble when giving her name.

"Oh, that sounds lovely," she said with an air that told him she'd be too busy to do that.

"How did you hear of Danger Bluff?" he asked.

"I saw an ad on the internet."

"Great. I'll tell the ad staff they're doing a great job," Hawking said as he pulled up to the front of the hotel. He jumped down from the jeep and rounded to help her out before grabbing her suitcase. "Let me walk you in to the desk."

"I can get there. Thank you for the ride."

He watched her eyes study his shirt as if she were memorizing his name. "My pleasure." He pulled his business card holder from his pocket and handed her a card. "If you have any concerns, let me know. I hope I'll run into you, Molly."

"Thank you, Mr. Winther."

"Call me, Hawking. This is an informal place."

"I've never met anyone named Hawking," she murmured, not moving. He wondered if she was delaying leaving him.

"Neither have I. Thanks to my mom, who lived near a reserve with red-tail hawks and the internet, there is now a Hawking. It means hawk-like or fierce."

"Are you fierce?" she asked.

"When it comes to something or someone important to me, I'm the fiercest."

"I'm glad to meet you then, Hawking. You're a good person to have on one's side." She tilted up her lips as she looked over her shoulder, then pulled her suitcase toward the open door.

"Call me if you need anything," Hawking called after her. *That smile.*

Chapter Four

Celeste almost ran into a man standing in the line at the reception desk. Jerking herself to a stop, she shook her head at her own silliness. Here she was, running for her life, or at least running away for her research's continued existence, and she wasn't paying attention to where she was headed.

"Hi!" a friendly woman called from behind the desk. Celeste pushed her thoughts from her head and moved forward.

"Hi. I'm Molly Smith. I'd like to prepay for seven days, although I'm planning to stay longer than that."

"I can certainly take care of that for you. We'll need a credit card on file," said the receptionist. Her nametag read Liz Foster.

"I don't use credit cards," Molly said bluntly, pulling out a thousand dollars she'd tucked into a pocket of her purse.

"The hotel policy is to have a credit card on file in case of incidentals," Liz informed her.

Celeste tightened her lips. "I don't have a credit card."

"I see. May I see your ID?" Liz requested as she waved toward a woman behind her.

"I don't drive," she lied. *Crap, crap, crap!* Celeste did not want anyone to know her real name. What was she going to do if they didn't let her stay here? She'd gotten lucky and jumped in the car of a rideshare driver who was dropping someone off.

"Hi, Liz. Is there something I can help you with?" the woman asked when she was near.

Celeste read her nametag, Sadie Miller, Front Desk Manager. Crossing her fingers behind her, Celeste hoped for the best.

"Sadie, this is Molly Smith," the clerk said. "She has a reservation and will stay for an extended vacation with us. Unfortunately, she doesn't have an ID or a credit card."

"Hi, Molly. I saw your reservation and noticed you didn't have a departure date. How would you like us to handle your stay?" Sadie asked with a smile.

"I would like to start with a thousand-dollar deposit on my account. I won't charge anything to the room and will add additional funds to my account as the room charges deplete this amount," Celeste proposed.

"I think we can make an exception to our normal procedure for Ms. Smith. Let me handle this account for you," Sadie suggested to the clerk before asking, "Could you run and grab some more keycards from the storeroom?"

"Good idea. We're running low."

When they were alone, Sadie smiled at Molly. "Sorry for the delay. Let me get you checked in."

In a matter of minutes, Sadie had counted the money and credited it to the account. She turned to grab a packet from the display behind her that was labeled Molly Smith. "Your room is on the fourth floor, and the elevators are to your left. Would you like help with your bags?"

"No, thank you."

Juggling the information packet, the keycard, her purse, and the rolling suitcase, Molly headed for the elevator. She wanted to get out of sight before the woman in charge changed her mind. Struggling to hold on to everything, she totally missed the familiar immense man in her path. *Wham!* She ran into a solid wall of muscle.

"Whoa!"

Large hands settled around her waist to steady her again. "This is getting to be a habit," he said with a laugh.

"Oh! I'm so sorry," she said, looking up.

"Let me help you to your room," Hawking said, setting her suitcase back on its wheels and picking up the packet. "I've got these two. Can I carry that bag for you?"

"I can't impose on you. I'm sure you have important security things to take care of," Celeste said quickly.

"Getting guests settled in their rooms is everyone's responsibility. We've only been open a week. We're all still pitching in to make sure everything runs smoothly. I'm glad to help." When the doors opened for the elevator, he ushered her inside. Unfortunately, they were the only ones in the car.

"Thank you." Celeste stood quietly. She wasn't good at social small talk. The silence felt awkward to her.

"Where are you visiting from?"

"The north island."

"What brings you to Danger Bluff?"

"I'm on vacation between jobs and wanted something in the wops."

"In the wops," Hawking repeated with a confused look.

"Oh, sorry. Kiwis use that for somewhere rural. I wanted

to relax away from the congestion of the city. You know, out in the wop wops."

"I like that. Wop wops. Danger Bluff is the perfect spot for a vacation," he assured her.

When the doors opened, she darted forward. "I can take it from here."

"Of course," he said, releasing the handle of her rolling case. "It's just two doors down that way," he said, pointing in the direction for her.

Heading down the hall, she could feel him watching her until she got to her door. Quickly, she waved her keycard over the lock and wrangled everything inside. Celeste threw the packet onto the bed and clicked the lock into place.

After setting her bag on the desk, Celeste sat down on the bed and replayed her interactions with the large, obviously former-military guy. His accent had given his U.S. citizenship away, and his reaction to wop wops told her he hadn't been in New Zealand for long. She attempted to keep her mind away from the feel of his hard body, but she failed miserably. *His muscles have muscles.*

"Okay. Enough drooling over the head of security. I need to get busy," Celeste announced to the empty room.

She retrieved her laptop and plugged it into the socket to charge. Celeste had used most of the battery studying and restudying the documentation that had gotten her fired. There was no way a non-science person had doctored this. It had to be someone with an insight into research and the study of diseases.

Unfortunately, that didn't narrow down her list of suspects. Virtually any research scientist in her company or its rivals could have changed the data. Even a competing drug company had the brainpower to make it look like she was totally off course.

She sat up straight as she pondered that idea. A drug company. They would have the motivation. A new possible cure or treatment that would make defeating cancer cells easier to isolate and kill would make the last-ditch medications that cost astronomical prices obsolete.

Celeste paced back and forth in her room as she tried to think. This didn't work. She needed to go for a run. Quickly, she put her suitcase on the bed and pulled out a set of running gear and her shoes. After changing her clothes, she sat down to put on her shoes and then looked around for a good hiding spot.

There! Finishing her bow, she stood and retrieved the hard drive from her bag. In a few seconds, she had it placed with the small coffee pot the hotel provided. The black case blended in perfectly with the metal frame around the device. No one would look at it twice.

Tucking her keycard into her bra, she walked out of the room and ran down the stairs instead of taking the elevator. Within a minute, she was outside.

Randomly choosing a sidewalk, she ran. Celeste decided to always turn right, figuring the paths looped around the property. She loved the grounds of the resort. People were everywhere, enjoying the beautiful flowers, pool, and the ocean. With a smile, she put running on the beach in the morning on her to-do list.

At the third possible right, she saw an employee-only area. Her sense of direction told her the route on the left would take her back to the main building. Not wanting to go back, Celeste turned to the right. She'd had enough of doing the right thing. *Look where that got me. Literally, on the run!*

Chuckling at herself, Celeste ran down the path. It was even more beautiful here. She had seen no one since turning in this direction. It was almost like having her own personal paradise. By the time she made the large loop around the resort, Celeste felt much better. She'd burnt off a lot of her nervous energy. Slowing to a walk, she cooled down on the path to the main building.

"You're making me look bad," Sadie called as Celeste walked into the reception area.

The woman who had helped her walked around the desk to fall into step with her. "I'm headed to talk to the employees in the laundry area."

"Oh! Thank you for saying that. Is there a machine available somewhere for guests to wash their clothes?" Celeste asked.

"There isn't a guest laundry facility, but there is a bag in the closet you can fill with clothes and drop off at the laundry. Come with me. I'll show you where it is. They'll deliver it back to your room the next day."

"That could work. Thank you." Celeste could try it once to see if she could afford the cost. She could always rinse out her underwear and hang them in the shower.

When they reached the laundry, a man at the entrance smiled at Sadie. "Hey, Sadie."

"Hi, Mark. This is a guest who's interested in sending things to the laundry. I'll leave you here, Molly, to get all the details."

"Hey, Molly. Here are a few extra bags. We just ask that you list the number of items you have on the bags. I'll remind you when you come down if it's not done. That helps us keep all your things together."

"Can I ask you what the cost is?"

"Wave your keycard over the sensor, and it will display the cost. It depends on what resort package you have."

Turning slightly, Celeste pulled her card from her sports bra and placed it close to the machine. *Free* popped up on the screen. "It doesn't cost anything?" she asked in amazement.

"Not for you. See you soon, Molly," Mark said, looking past her to help the next customer.

Celeste whirled, and *Bam!* Those powerful hands spanned her waist to help her keep her balance. She raised her head, and her eyes locked with deep brown ones filled with laughter.

"I am so sorry," she apologized. How could she keep running into this man?

"You have to be bruised by now," he said with a laugh.

"You are hard," she stated before feeling her face flame with embarrassment. She looked down to break their eye contact and then realized what she was looking at and slapped her hand over her eyes. "That's not what I meant."

"Here's your laundry, Hawking."

"Thanks, Mark."

Hawking guided her away from the laundry area with a hand at the small of her back and into a small alcove. "You can lower your hand now. Mark didn't see anything. He went to the back to get my clothes."

"Could you just point me at a wall and go somewhere safe? I'll count to a hundred and go hide in my room," Celeste said, wishing the ground would open under her feet.

"Not going to happen, Little girl. I need to keep you where I can see you so you don't run into anything harder than me and get injured." He chuckled. "What are you doing for dinner?"

"Dinner?" Her mind seized on that instead of focusing on the endearment, Little girl. He couldn't know—could he?

Chapter Five

"Dinner. We eat and relax. After all, it looks like we're destined to run into each other," Hawking teased.

"I am so sorry. Usually, I'm not so uncoordinated." Inwardly, she rolled her eyes at that statement. When it came to working in a lab, she was incredibly on point and skilled. She could roll back and forth between a microscope and her computer with ease.

"I think something is telling us we need to get to know each other. Have dinner with me. We'll go to The Market. It's an outside café. There will be families and couples. The food is everything from fish and chips to salads with New Zealand wines and craft beer to top things off."

Her stomach growled loudly. This time, Celeste slapped her hand over her flat tummy. The laughter in his eyes was irresistible. "Okay. My stomach is a traitor and has outed me for missing breakfast and lunch."

"Let's go change," he suggested and wrapped an arm around her to safely guide her to the elevator.

A crowd was getting on the elevator, and Celeste couldn't

believe she was holding her breath to make sure he made it in. But the gust she exhaled when he stepped inside showed her how much she wanted him around. Leaning against the wall, she waited to get to her floor as the elevator stopped at each level to let people out. Finally, they reached the fourth floor, and she pushed away from the wall to walk out after the last couple.

"Aren't you getting out?" she asked.

"I'm on the fifth floor. Some employees live up there. I'll meet you here by the elevator in an hour."

"Thirty minutes?" she asked, and her stomach growled again.

"Want to make it twenty?"

"Please," she said with a laugh.

"Twenty minutes," he agreed.

She stood and watched as the elevator doors closed. Shaking herself, she fled the short distance down the hallway and opened her door. Everything was exactly as she had left it.

She ran into the shower. Fifteen minutes later, her hair was almost dry. Celeste had a relatively clean pair of jeans and a shirt on. Of course, she hadn't brought much makeup. She made do with a tube of lip gloss and mascara. Making a face at herself in the mirror, Celeste gave up trying to make herself something she wasn't.

Staring at her reflection in the bathroom mirror, Celeste recalled the last time she'd gotten all dressed up. She'd had a blast at the fancy event her ex-company had thrown. With the goal of asking wealthy community members for donations, her boss had stressed that everyone needed to attend. Celeste hadn't recognized herself after her makeover. Her hairdresser had been itching to show her how to put on makeup. That woman obviously had serious talent in making her look so good.

After the gala, Celeste had turned down requests for dates from single—and some married—men from every department. Finally, when they'd seen she was not going to recreate the woman they'd all stared at, the invitations had dried up. At least she knew Hawking hadn't seen that woman, which meant he had asked her to dinner without even knowing how she could look after an afternoon of pampering.

The idea made her feel desirable, and Lord knew it had been a while since she'd felt anything resembling desirable. She shook the thought from her head. "He only asked you to dinner. He's probably just being polite. You have no reason to think he's interested in you," she mumbled to herself.

She flushed as she remembered glancing down at his, uh, his crotch earlier. Had he *actually* been hard? Maybe he was interested in her.

Stepping out of her room, she saw Hawking standing patiently at the elevator. He was dressed in jeans that hugged the corded muscles of his thighs and a red T-shirt that revealed the power of his arms and shoulders. She tried not to notice anything else, keeping her eyes on his.

"I'm ready."

He punched the down button. "Perfect. Let's go try out the Danger Bluff chefs at the restaurant near the dock. We've been enjoying the food here in the main building for days. It'll be good to get out for a change," he shared.

"Who's we?" she asked curiously as they stepped into the elevator.

"There's a small management team here that has worked together to get ready for the opening. We get along well and have the same goals, so we decided to have dinner together every night."

"Oh. I'm interrupting your plans."

"They'll be fine without me. I sent my update to the tech guy. He'll share my notes from today," Hawking said.

As they stepped off the elevator into a swirl of excited guests, Hawking made a motion with his hand, indicating which way to head. As he created a path for her to walk through, Celeste tried everything to keep her eyes on his back as she followed him, but his toned ass kept drawing her gaze. After almost running into his back twice when he stopped to answer a question or allow someone to cross their path, Celeste placed a hand on his midback so she'd have warning every time he paused.

"I am determined to slam into you," she said, laughing.

"Anytime, Little girl," he answered as the path cleared, and he slowed to guide her up next to him.

He led her into a large restaurant with the walls pushed back on three sides to allow air to flow through. Lush foliage inside provided privacy between the tables. The hostess took them to an empty table on the edge of the restaurant and left them with the menus.

"I've heard from the locals that work at the hotel that the crayfish are amazing. I understand that's a New Zealand dish I should try? The restaurant buys the seafood from local merchants," he shared.

"Why do you call me Little girl?" she blurted, ignoring his question.

"Am I wrong? Something inside me is telling me to pay attention to you."

"Maybe because I keep running into you," she suggested, trying to make a joke.

"No. That's not it. It's the Daddy inside me that's sure you're mine."

She stared at him in shock. Did he just tell her he was a Daddy? And he thinks she's his? "Does it actually work like that?"

"It does if you're lucky. I'm feeling like I won the lottery."

"Would you like anything to drink?" the server asked with a smile. "I'm Luka. I'll take care of you tonight. Hi, Hawking."

"Hi, Luka."

Hawking turned to Celeste and asked, "Do you enjoy wine?"

"Yes?" she answered as her thoughts swirled around in her brain.

"Bring us some water and a bottle of house rosé," Hawking requested.

When Luka departed, Hawking placed an open hand on the table, silently asking for hers. Celeste nestled hers in his. He closed his fingers around hers and squeezed gently. "I've been looking for my Little girl for years. Can you be brave for me?"

"How did you know?" she whispered, leaning forward.

"In here," Hawking tapped his chest with his free hand. "Can you feel it, too?"

She nodded without meaning to. There were so many things going on right now. How could she deal with dating a Daddy on top of everything else? "This isn't a good time for me. My life is complicated," she whispered.

"I won't let you run away. Instead, I'm going to help you."

"Help me?" she echoed.

Luka returned at that moment. "I've got all the help you need," he teased as he uncorked the wine and poured a sample for Hawking to sample.

"That will do nicely, Luka."

As he filled her glass with the beautiful pink beverage, Luka asked, "Do you have any questions about the menu?"

"Does the chef have any specials tonight?" Hawking asked.

"How does honey-glazed salmon with mixed vegetables sound?" Luka asked with a smile.

"I'll take that," Celeste responded. It was much easier to choose that than search the menu for something different to eat. She definitely couldn't concentrate on all the options.

"Lamb shank for me, please."

"Oh, you'll enjoy those choices," Luka said with a smile as he departed to put their orders in.

"How are you going to help me?" she asked as soon as Luka was out of range.

"I'm going to keep you safe, Celeste."

She shifted to bolt from her chair at his use of her real name, panic crawling up her spine. How had he known? He tightened his fingers to hold her hand pressed against the table.

"Your running is done, Celeste."

"You know that makes you sound like a bad guy," she whispered. It would be much easier to run away than to trust that he was on her side. She frowned. "How do you know I'm on the run? How do you know my name?"

"It's a long story. The important thing right now is for you to know that nothing bad is going to happen to you. You're safe with me and at the resort. I'll make sure of it."

She stared at him, breathing heavily. This made no sense. How could he know? She shuddered at the possibilities and narrowed her gaze at him. "Do you work for Dr. Hughes?" That had to be it. He worked for her boss at the lab, and Dr. Hughes had sent him to... To what? Keep her quiet?

Hawking shook his head. "No, Little girl. I work for the man who owns this resort. My job is to keep you safe."

She trembled. "How do I know I can trust you?"

"I bet you've been on edge for days. Stop thinking with your brain and feel. How does your Little feel?" he asked quietly.

After a few long seconds, she felt her racing heartbeat slow. "Like you're going to keep me safe, and I can trust you." She couldn't explain it, but she felt drawn to him in a way she'd never experienced. *This isn't a romance novel*, she silently chided herself.

"That's exactly what I plan to do. Can you relax so we can get some fuel inside you?"

Feeling like his steady presence grounded her, she settled back against the chair and asked, "How did I ever find you?"

"How about if we decide we have a fairy godmother with a wand?"

Her lips curved in a smile as she imagined a small, winged figure darting around Hawking's huge bulk.

"She better not run into you. She'll knock herself out."

His chuckle made her laugh. Whatever it was that linked them together, she felt better with him nearby. Deciding she needed to trust someone, Celeste chose to rely on him.

Chapter Six

Her yawn made him signal for the bill. "You're exhausted, Little girl. It's time for bed." He signed the tab and escorted her back toward the hotel. She scooted closer to him in the dark as they entered the main building.

"Sorry. I just can't stay awake. It's like eight o'clock. This is ridiculous."

"I would bet you haven't slept for a few days while you were traveling," he guessed.

"No." Every time she'd fallen asleep, she'd jolted awake, feeling like someone was about to get her.

"Then, tonight, you go to bed early."

"I won't sleep well," she said sadly. "I always think they're going to find me." Her breath hitched as those words left her mouth. Even though Hawking seemed to mysteriously know she was in trouble, he surely didn't know all the details of her predicament.

Hawking wrapped an arm around her and did not comment on her statement except to whisper, "I've got you."

As they entered the main building, Hawking guided her

through the vacationing couples and families. Keeping her tucked against his powerful body, he didn't ask questions but held her close until they exited the elevator on the fourth floor. Another couple preceded them out of the elevator and walked past her door.

Celeste opened her door and tugged Hawking inside. "This is going to sound awful. I'm not putting the moves on you, but could you sleep here tonight?"

"Do you think you could sleep better if you have someone here?"

"Not *someone*. I know I would be able to keep from waking up every five minutes if *you* were here," she said, stressing the word you. *Please say yes*. She would be mortified if he turned her down.

"I will need to get up early for work," he warned her.

"That's okay. I like to work in the mornings."

"Go get ready for bed, Little girl," Hawking instructed.

"Really? You'll stay?"

"I'll stay tonight." He was smiling.

"Thank you."

She bustled around to find her nightshirt and darted into the bathroom to shower, brush her teeth, and potty. When she returned to the main room, Hawking was sitting on the office chair, looking through his phone.

"You look ready for bed," he said as he stood to pull back the covers. "In you go, Little girl."

Celeste dropped her dirty clothes on her suitcase and carefully slid into bed. She never wore panties to bed, so she had to be very careful not to flash him as she got under the covers.

When she was settled, she quickly snagged her stuffie from the pillow and pulled her under the covers, grateful that Hawking didn't comment on her need to have Hades close.

As she watched, Hawking turned off all the lights except for the one on the other side of the bed. He laid down on top of the covers with his head propped up. Tapping on his phone, he pulled something up before looking over at her.

"Time to close your eyes, Celeste. Let's take three deep breaths together. Count to three on the inhale and six on the exhale. Ready?"

She didn't really know what she was doing, but Celeste followed his lead as he breathed in, chanting, "One, Two, Three." And then she slowly let it out as he announced the numbers to six. By the third time they repeated that, she was focused totally on her breath.

"Keep breathing like that, Celeste."

She nodded and saw him tap the screen on his phone. To her delight, he announced, "Chapter one."

The story was wonderful. The characters came to life as he read the tale of the princess who went on a glorious adventure. Celeste found she could imagine everything that happened easier if she closed her eyes. His deep voice wrapped around her. Feeling secure for the first time in days, Celeste drifted to sleep.

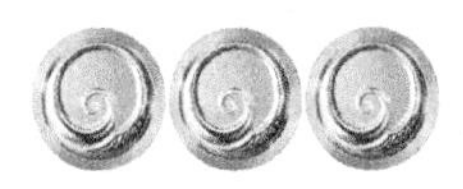

"Good morning, Princess."

"I'm not a princess. I'm a scientist," she mumbled and shimmied closer to the heat radiating her way. A warm band wrapped around her waist, tugging her a bit closer. "Mmm."

"I have to leave, Little girl. All the guests in the hotel will be up and wandering around."

"Guests?" she echoed, trying to process what those words

meant. Slowly, she blinked open her eyes to see a handsome face just a few inches from hers. "Hawking?"

"Hi, Cuddle Bug."

She couldn't argue with that. He'd stayed exactly where he had stretched out last night. She had snuggled as close as possible overnight. She wrinkled her nose. "Sorry?"

"No apologies needed, Little girl. I'll never be unhappy to hold you in my arms. Did you sleep well?"

Nodding, Celeste realized she hadn't woken up once all night. Hawking had kept all the worries away. Having him there as her personal security guard solved her problem of not getting any rest.

"Thank you. I feel so much better. Did you get to sleep at all?" she asked.

"I always sleep lightly, but you only snored a couple of times."

"I don't snore," she said, appalled.

"You're right. You don't. I was teasing you, CB."

"CB? What does that mean? My initials?" she asked, trying to fully wake up and follow his words.

"Cuddle Bug. Though it does match your name, Miss Celeste Blanke."

"Is that a coincidence, or did you plot a nickname that makes my initials?" she asked as she scooted to the edge of the bed.

"I did not go through the Daddy list of possible names for a Little girl and find one that included a C and a B. I could just call you Cuddle Bug if you'd prefer."

"Out in public?" she said, aghast, as she sat up.

"You'd prefer CB?" he asked, teasing. "Then it will be a secret that you love to sleep right next to your Daddy."

Celeste stared at him with wide eyes as he hauled her back against him. Her nightshirt bunched around her legs, and she stopped trying to get away as she realized her efforts were making it inch upward. "Mmm. Don't you need to go to work?"

"You don't snore, but you do talk in your sleep," he informed her.

"What did I say?" Celeste didn't even try to deny it. Her university roommate had teased her incessantly about the things she'd mumbled in her sleep.

"You might have mentioned a couple of times you wanted to kiss me," he shared.

"That didn't happen!"

"It did. You were obviously thinking about pressing your lips to mine."

Her focus narrowed to his full lips. She knew she'd said that in her sleep because she'd thought of it several times during dinner. Her gaze darted back to link with his. Had she talked about other things she wanted to do with him?

His slow wink told her she'd talked about those as well. Instead of denying everything, Celeste leaned forward to kiss his lips. He responded, allowing her to control the kiss until she licked the seam of his lips to ask for entrance.

Hawking seized control of the exchange. His hand cupped the back of her head, holding her in place as he explored her mouth as if he had all the time in the world and wanted to savor her. She wrapped her arms around his neck and held on.

Her wordless sound of protest when he lifted his head made him smile. "I know, Cuddle Bug. I don't want to go either. But I have to go to work. Why don't you try to fall back asleep?"

"That's never going to happen," she stated emphatically. An image of her buzzing vibrator on her bed popped into her mind, causing a shiver to go through her.

"Whatever just popped into your mind, erase it, Little girl. You're safe here with me."

"I can't believe you're a Daddy."

"I'm not just *a* Daddy; I'm your Daddy."

"You can't be sure of that."

"Oh, I'm sure. I just need to help you be sure. I've got to get to work. Give me another kiss, and I'll watch for you around the resort."

"I'll probably work in my room," she said, looking around at the area that felt very safe now.

"I don't want you to spend all your time in your room. How about we have dinner together?"

"I would love that." She beamed at him.

"It's a date, Cuddle Bug."

He rolled off the bed and stopped to kiss her lightly before heading for the door with his phone in his hand. "Call me if you have any problems."

"I don't have a phone. Well, I'm not turning mine on."

"I'll take care of that for you. In the meantime, use the room phone. Will anyone call you here at the resort?"

"No. No one knows I'm here."

"I'll make sure the front desk doesn't connect anyone to the room," he continued. He also padded over to the desk, wrote something down on the hotel memo pad, and held it up. "My personal number. I'll have breakfast sent up to you in one hour. It'll be safe to open the door at that time."

Celeste turned to look at the time and heard the click as he left, locking the door behind him. A smile curved her lips, and she stood up to stretch. She'd felt so secure last night. Crossing her fingers, she hoped she could get him to stay again.

Chapter Seven

After jogging up one floor to his apartment, Hawking showered and put on fresh clothes before heading down to the security office. He ordered breakfast to be delivered to Celeste's room and to him.

"Anyone going into town today?" he asked his team through his earpiece.

"I'm headed there to pick up a couple who want to go scuba diving," Caesar answered within seconds.

"Could you go early and pick up a disposable phone for me?"

"Of course."

"Thank you, Caesar."

"We missed you last night at dinner," Rocco teased.

"I had a much prettier face to look at than you guys. I'll get you caught up soon," Hawking promised.

He had read all the evening security reports and had decided to check the perimeter of the resort when his phone buzzed. Hawking tapped the screen and brought the cell to his ear. "Magnus? How are things in the basement?"

"One of the front desk clerks just notified me of a phone call that came for Molly Smith last night. It must have been while you were at dinner. Seeing the block on receiving calls listed for the room, she reported that there were no guests by that name but jotted the note down when he insisted on leaving a message. Unfortunately, she didn't take time to notify me until a second fishing call came in this morning."

"Fuck! Why didn't she send a message immediately?" Hawking asked, standing up to go to the reception area.

"Sadie is addressing the lapse in time as a training issue," Magnus assured him.

"Damn right, it's a training issue."

"In her defense, the new receptionist has no idea Celeste is in any trouble. It's not like we've announced it to the entire staff. Plus, Smith is the most common last name in New Zealand, Hawking. It's very possible that they weren't looking for your Little, hiding under Molly Smith. The clerk did follow the guidelines you set into place and gave the routine answer that she couldn't access that information to confirm whether Danger Bluff had a reservation or not under that name and to suggest he contact his friend on their cell phone."

"They're tracking her. If they have access to facial identification from the ferry or other sources, whoever is behind this is extremely powerful," Hawking pointed out. "And we have no idea who or what to look for." His frustration mounted as he wondered if his Little girl was in her room right now. He hoped so. He didn't like this development.

"I would suggest you move her up to the fifth floor. That gives her another level of security while we see what their next move is."

Hawking nodded to himself. "Good call. Keep your eyes open, Magnus."

"As always, Hawking. Go get your Little. I'm watching her floor, and there's an employee with a cart, knocking on doors."

Disconnecting, Hawking jogged to the elevator and celebrated his luck when the doors opened immediately. He rode it up to the fourth floor. As he exited the elevator, he noticed the housekeeping cart standing at Celeste's door. He quickened his steps and saw to his horror that his Little stood at the door with a stack of fresh towels in her hand as she chatted with the employee.

"Good morning, ladies." He scanned the employee's name tag and noted that the picture and the woman's appearance didn't match.

Swearing inside his head, Hawking thought quickly to protect his Little and get the fake employee away from Celeste. "The head of housekeeping requested all employees return to speak with her. There was something about a batch of towels that received the wrong softener. Nothing dangerous but not Danger Bluff level comfort. I better take these."

He plucked the towels from Celeste's arms. "I'll make sure you get a new set as soon as possible, Miss."

Turning back to the employee, he suggested, "I'm headed down there. Let's go check in, and you can restock the cart."

The employee stared at him with wide eyes.

"Sorry to disturb you," he said to Celeste when she continued to stand there, urging her to escape into her room with his warning gaze. To his relief, she nodded and stepped back into the room.

"What's wrong with the fabric softener?" the employee said nervously as she pushed the cart toward the closest elevator.

"Who knows? We'll take the service elevator at the rear

of the hotel." Hawking nodded that direction and watched the woman stop uncertainly as if she didn't know where that elevator was. "It's easy to get turned around in here. It's that way."

Once she was in the elevator, he sent an alert to his security team and the other five Daddies.

When the doors opened on the first floor, the "employee" looked at the three large men skidding to a stop in security polos and held up her hands. "They wired money to my bank account an hour ago. I didn't do anything wrong. I just came and knocked on doors."

"Hawking, this was on the cart." Rocco held up a cell phone displaying a picture of Celeste in her lab coat. It looked like something that would appear on an ID badge.

"That's the woman they were looking for," the fake employee stated.

"Did you notify them she was here?" Hawking asked.

"I didn't yet. I won't."

"Trespassing. Stealing company equipment. Stealing an ID," Hawking ticked off the crimes she had committed.

"It's public property. I didn't trespass."

"It's private property accessible only by employees and guests. You are neither," Hawking corrected her with a pointed glare that made her scramble to excuse her actions.

"I didn't steal anything. The cart was parked in that unlocked room downstairs. I just pushed it upstairs. The ID badge was in the top drawer," the woman said as if that excused her behavior.

"She started on the fourth floor," Magnus said into Hawking's earpiece.

"Why did you start on the fourth floor?" Hawking asked.

"I... It's the top one. I was just working my way down," the imposter said quickly.

Hawking stared at her. "Who contacted you?"

"I don't know. They said they would help me get medicine that could help my son. He's so sick," the woman babbled as her eyes filled with tears.

"Cancer?" Hawking guessed.

"Yes. The doctors have warned they're running out of options."

"If you found this woman, what were you to do?" Hawking grilled her.

"I was supposed to send an alert back to that message. I can just say I didn't find her," the woman suggested, obviously petrified now that she had gotten caught.

"Give me your real driver's license," Hawking insisted, holding out his hand.

She immediately produced it. Hawking knew she was frightened, and that was a good thing. He also sympathized with her motivation. He would have done anything for a chance at hope for his mother.

Taking a picture, he sent the image of the ID to Magnus. Ten minutes later, Magnus spoke into the teams' earpieces.

"She checks out. All the background information is correct. I've scanned her cell phone records, and she was contacted by someone supposedly working with the hospital. I'd say keep her for a while so they think she's actually looking for Celeste. Then have her text and release her."

The other team members echoed the decision to release her.

Hawking looked at her pale face and said, "Your story checks out. I'm sorry about your son. The people who are searching for this woman are not good people. Helping them will endanger her and will not cure your son."

"I'll send them a message that I didn't find her," the woman promised.

"We'll let you do that in a couple of hours. It's vital that they think you've completed your mission," Hawking shared.

"Can I check on my son?" she asked urgently.

"Put your phone on speaker so I can hear. Then I'll hold on to the phone until it's time to text."

Two hours later, Hawking was at the front desk monitoring every person coming into the building when a limousine pulled up to the front of the hotel. A few moments later, the driver stepped out of his car and entered. "Is there a Hawking Winther here?"

"Yes, can I help you?" The hairs on the back of Hawking's neck stood on end.

"Here."

Hawking unfolded the note that the chauffeur handed him and read:

> *This car will take the woman and her son to the largest private cancer institute in New Zealand, where he will receive the best care. I will cover the bills.*

It was signed with the golden token.

A burden lifted from Hawking's shoulders. He'd battled himself all day long. Celeste had to be his first priority, but he sympathized so much with this mom who chose to do anything to help her child.

Walking back to the room where she sat surrounded by several people watching her closely, Hawking handed her the note. "This is from the owner of the hotel." He watched her read it. And reread it.

Her eyes swam with tears as she darted a glance at the large man towering over her. "Does he mean it?"

"There's a limo outside waiting to go pick up your son." Hawking held out her phone. "You can send that text now."

"I would've lied about finding that woman, anyway. I'm so ashamed that I could've endangered someone else," she told him.

He simply nodded, then watched her type out a message and send it. *She is not here.*

There was no response.

"They weren't going to help him anyway, were they?" she asked.

"Probably not."

Shaking her head, the woman stood and gestured with the note. "Thank you."

"May they help your son," Hawking wished the woman well and escorted her to the front door. "Do not return here."

"Yes, sir."

Bowing her head to look down at the sidewalk as she walked out of the building, Hawking watched her go before turning to go check on Celeste.

Chapter Eight

Giggling caught his ear as he got off the elevator. It was infectious, and he smiled as he realized the sound came from more than one Little girl. As he walked down the hall, the laughter grew louder. He knocked on the door and heard it go silent inside.

"It's me. Hawking."

The door flew open, and Celeste wrapped her arms around his neck, pressing her body close. Hawking simply encircled her slender waist and lifted her toes from the carpeting as he walked forward. The door slammed shut behind them.

"Hi, Sadie," he said, giving the other Little a glance.

"Hi, Hawking. I took my lunch break here with Celeste," Sadie said easily.

"Is everything okay?" Celeste asked, leaning back to peek up at him.

"I hope so. The woman was coerced in hopes of someone helping her son."

"That's awful," Sadie exclaimed.

"Cancer?" Celeste asked.

Hawking nodded to confirm her guess. "The owner of the resort is funding the son's treatment. She reported that she hadn't found you to the people that sent her here."

"That's good, isn't it?" Celeste asked.

"Maybe. You're not safe on this floor, though. We'll move you to the fifth floor as soon as you can be ready."

"I just have my computer and my suitcase. Want me to throw everything together now?" she asked.

"Yes. I'll breathe easier when you're secured."

Sadie helped her gather her few things and return them to her purse and suitcase. The kind woman didn't chatter as they packed everything, but she did comment on Celeste's black cat stuffie's name.

"Hades? Isn't that the god of the underworld? Isn't that scary to sleep with?" Sadie asked.

"*My* Hades is a girl. She's still the ruler of all the scary stuff. That's the best part because she keeps everything bad away from me," Celeste explained.

"That is really smart. They have to do what she says," Sadie said with a grin.

"Do you have everything?" Hawking asked.

Celeste looked around and then dashed over to the coffee pot and grabbed something from next to it, which she added to her purse. It looked like a hard drive. Had she been hiding it? He wondered if it held the unaltered data from her cancer research.

With Magnus watching from the basement to give them the green light by text, the trio dashed into the elevator.

"There isn't a fifth-floor button," Celeste pointed out. She then fell quiet as Hawking placed his thumb on a section of the wall above the numbers.

He glanced at Celeste and winked. "Magic," he whispered.

The elevator glided upward and opened on the top floor where Hawking once again used his thumbprint to open a door that led into a large gathering area with comfortable seating and a huge TV. He knew this was all a shock to Celeste.

Sadie ran across the room to point at the door with a penguin on the front. "This is where I stay. I love penguins. Your door is there." She pointed at another door before looking at her watch. "I have to get back to the front area. Will Celeste be at dinner tonight?"

"She will," Hawking assured her.

"See you there," Sadie said and dashed forward to give Celeste a hug. "Don't worry. Hawking and the guys will keep you safe."

"I guess we'll have to put a black cat on my door," Hawking said with a laugh.

"I'm staying with you?" Celeste whispered.

"Yes. There's a separate room for you if you wish to sleep by yourself," he assured her.

Immediately, she shook her head. "I want to sleep with you and Hades."

"I'd love that, too. Let me show you our area," Hawking said, wheeling her suitcase into the large bedroom. "The dresser drawers on the right are empty, and there's space in the closet. Unpack and settle in before dinner. The bathroom is through there."

"What's through there?" Celeste asked, pointing at an adjoining door.

"That's the other bedroom. A type of playroom."

"Like for video games?"

He chuckled. "No, Little girl. A playroom for you. A

place where you can be Little." He hoped she was ready to hear all this.

Her eyes went wide. "Can I see it?"

"You can do more than that. You can explore anything, Little girl."

He opened the door and escorted her inside. He hadn't done much to prepare this room because he hadn't known until two days ago that Celeste was coming, let alone that she was his Little girl. "There's a desk. You could claim that for your own if you wish."

Celeste darted forward to set her oversized purse on the flat surface. "Mine."

Hawking had to laugh. "Yours, CB."

She turned around in a circle several times, taking everything in. The day bed, the dresser, the rocking chair, the bookshelf. "But..."

He chuckled again as he stepped behind her and set his hands on her shoulders. "I've been looking for my Little girl for a long time, Celeste. I was getting prepared."

She twisted around, causing his hands to drop to her hips. "I don't understand what's happening. You haven't told me how you know my name or about my problems. And why do you care?"

He pulled her closer, flattening his chest to hers. She felt so good against him. Even though he'd slept next to her on her bed last night, he hadn't been this close to her yet. He really wanted to kiss her again, too. Her full lips were so tempting.

"Let's start with the last question," he said. "I care because you're mine, CB. I'm pretty sure I knew that before you even arrived, but the moment I set eyes on you, it was confirmed."

Her jaw fell open.

"As for the rest, all I can say is that the owner of this resort, Baldwin Kingsley, knows a lot of things. He's made it his mission to help people. I can't say how he knew about your problems, but he assigned me to keep you safe."

She licked those full lips, still staring at him.

"What I know for certain is that I'd really like to kiss you before I get back to work. You can take some time to settle in here. I'll leave you a list of the local stores. Go to their websites and pick out some things to make this room special. Tonight, we can place a few orders. Tomorrow, I'll go into town and pick everything up."

She gasped. "I can't do that. I'm afraid to use my credit cards. Someone could track me with them. Plus, I just got fired. I don't have money for frivolous things."

He pulled her even closer. "I do, CB. *I'll* furnish this room. Not you. Keep your credit cards put away, but for the record, your old boss has obviously already found you. Your location is not a secret any longer."

"How do you think he found me?"

"I'm not sure yet, Cuddle Bug. I'd like you to tell your story to the entire team this evening. It will help us decide what to do next. Okay?"

She nodded. "Yes."

"Now, you ignored the important part," he pointed out.

"What was that?" Her brow furrowed.

"Are you going to kiss me?"

She shook her head and giggled. "No. *You're* going to kiss *me*."

Thank God. Hawking leaned down as she tipped her head to one side and claimed her sweet lips with his own. She tasted sweet and tart, like...gummy bears?

When she made a little whimper and rose onto her toes, he deepened the kiss. She was made for him. He'd already known that, but this kiss confirmed everything. It was so much more intense than the one they'd exchanged this morning.

Before he could get too carried away, he broke the kiss. "What did you girls eat for lunch, CB?"

She giggled, her cheeks turning red. "Sadie brought sandwiches and apples."

"And then?" he prompted.

"Uh, well, she might have also had gummy bears in her pocket, but I don't think you should tell her Daddy."

"Is that so?" He couldn't keep from grinning. He loved everything about this exchange. He loved the fact that Celeste felt safe enough to let her Little out so totally in front of him. He loved that she knew she and Sadie had done something naughty. But most of all, he loved how she shifted her weight back and forth from one foot to the other. Being naughty made her fidget.

"You won't tell him, will you?" she asked, her eyes wide again.

"Oh, I'm pretty sure Sadie pulled that stunt on purpose. You don't have to worry about me outing her. She was hoping you would."

Celeste gasped. "Why would she do that?"

He chuckled. "Because she's been working really hard around here, and I'm sure she needs the release."

Celeste frowned. "What release?"

"The one she's going to get from Rocco when he finds out she ate gummy bears without permission."

Her frown deepened.

Hawking slid his hand down to her bottom and gave it a pat. "A spanking, Little girl."

She flinched adorably. "Really? Do Daddies really spank Little girls in real life? I thought that was only in books."

He smiled at her naiveté. "Daddies definitely spank Little girls in real life, CB. Have you ever had a Daddy before?" He already suspected he knew the answer.

She shook her head. "No. I only realized I liked being Little from reading books. I've never told anyone before you."

"You didn't tell me, either. I figured it out because I have Little girl radar."

She giggled again. "Are you going to spank me for eating gummy bears, too?"

He patted her cute bottom again. "No, Little girl. Not right now. We didn't discuss any rules before you ate those gummy bears."

She chewed on her bottom lip for a moment before releasing it. "But I knew it was naughty because Sadie told me," she whispered.

He laughed. "Okay, Little girl. That sounds like a challenge."

She shook her head vehemently. "No, Sir."

He planted another kiss on her sweet lips. "How about if you call me Daddy?"

She swallowed hard. "I just met you yesterday, and I have a pile of problems you do not want to get involved with." She started to pull away from him.

"Uh-uh, Little girl. Don't try to wiggle free of me." He held her tighter. "You know in your heart that it doesn't matter how long we've known each other, don't you?" He lifted a brow.

She sighed. "Yes, Sir," she murmured.

He lifted his brow higher.

She licked those pretty lips again. "Yes, Daddy."

"Do you think I'd be a very good Daddy if I turned you away when you needed my help?"

"No, but—"

He shook his head and cut her off. "No buts, Little girl. As a Daddy, my job is to keep you safe, and that's what I'm going to do."

"Okay, Daddy," she whispered in the cutest Little voice he'd ever heard. His heart was so full.

He patted her bottom one more time. "I'll be happy to spank this naughty little bottom sometime soon. I know you're curious. But not right now."

She nodded, her pretty cheeks turning ten shades of pink again.

It was obvious she'd never had a Daddy before, so everything she knew or thought she knew had come from books and probably the internet.

Unable to resist, Hawking kissed her again and released her. "Do you have a laptop in your bag, CB?" He nodded toward the large purse she'd set on the desk.

"Yes, but I turned it off and haven't used it for several days because I was afraid Dr. Hughes might be able to track me somehow. I was paranoid. That's why I turned off my phone, too."

"That was a smart move, Celeste. I'm proud of you. Can I take your computer downstairs and let Magnus look at it? He might be able to see if someone is tracking it. Your phone, too."

She rushed over to her bag and pulled out both items. "You're going to want this as well," she said, holding up a hard drive.

Hawking pocketed it.

"You won't destroy any data on that, will you?"

"No. Never. Magnus is a computer genius. He'll preserve it. I promise. Meanwhile, he'll give you a temporary laptop to use."

She blew out a relieved breath, grabbed another box from

the bag, and held it up. "Sadie brought me this new phone when she came for lunch. I didn't open it yet."

Hawking took the box and opened it up. "Let's get it set up for you. I'll put in all our numbers so you can contact any one of us if you need something. Though I expect you to try me first."

She twisted her fingers together while she watched him set it up. "Thank you," she whispered.

When he was finished and looked at her, tears were running down her cheeks. He set the phone on the desk and pulled her into his arms again. "It's all going to be okay, Little girl. I promise."

God, he hoped so.

Chapter Nine

"Where are we going?" Celeste asked that evening after Hawking came to get her. She'd spent the afternoon using his laptop to peruse the local stores for things for her playroom, but she hadn't been able to put anything in the cart.

She couldn't spend his money, and she certainly couldn't spend her own, so she'd looked and lusted after a lot of things as if she were living in a make-believe world.

"To join the team for dinner." He glanced at the computer she sat in front of. A moment later, he frowned. "There's nothing in the cart."

She tipped her head back to look up at him. "I couldn't, but it was fun looking."

He turned her desk chair to fully face him and tipped her chin back. "Celeste, you need pretty things for this playroom. It doesn't have bedding or toys or books or games. Nothing on the walls. It's boring. It's a blank slate, waiting for a Little girl to outfit it."

She glanced around. He was right, but still... "I can't spend your money."

"Sure, you can, CB. If you don't, you'll hurt my feelings." He gave her a huge fake pout, even batting his eyes.

She giggled. "You look silly."

"Daddies are sometimes silly. Now, let's go downstairs to eat with the team. After dinner, you can tell your story." He helped her stand and turned her toward the living room.

She glanced back toward the special room. She hadn't told him, but she'd spent a lot of time picturing what it would look like if she really did buy all the things she'd looked at. "Am I going to sleep in the playroom, Daddy?"

"That's up to you, Cuddle Bug. You said before you wanted to sleep with Daddy, but if you're not ready to do that, you may sleep in here as long as you like."

She shook her head. "I want to sleep with you, please, but why do you have a bed in here then?"

He led her to the door. "For naps and times when you want to be alone."

"I've been alone for a long time," she told him as they left the apartment. Suddenly, she didn't want to be alone any longer. It made her feel sad.

"You're not alone now, Little girl," he said gently as he guided her out to the elevator. While they waited, he took her chin. "You'll never be alone again."

She swallowed over the lump in her throat and stared at him. It was hard to believe he was serious or that any of this was real.

"You'll see, CB," he said as if he'd read her mind. He threaded their fingers together as they entered the elevator.

"Are we going to the restaurant?"

"Nope. We're going to the basement."

"Basement?"

He set his thumb on the pad in the elevator, and the door closed just like it had earlier to bring them to the fifth floor.

"Yes. Wait until you see it. It's like a command center. It's also a safe room. It's where the team touches base and works when we're not out doing something for the resort."

"You keep referring to the group as a team like you're in the military," she pointed out.

He shrugged. "At one point, we all served in the military, but we're our own team now. Kingsley brought us together to complete whatever missions he assigns to us."

The doors opened before she could question him further. She stepped out of the elevator into a world she hadn't known existed under the resort's main building. "Wow."

To say it was a command center was an understatement. It looked like something out of a movie. There was an entire bank of computers and monitors with so many flashing screens.

Hawking set a hand on the small of her back, encouraging her to step farther into the room. "Let me introduce you to Magnus."

Just then, the man sitting in a fancy chair in front of the computer station spun around so he faced her. It was hard to see exactly what he looked like with his ball cap pulled down, shading his face, but she could tell he was built. All of the six men in the room who were looking at her were huge and muscular.

As they approached, Hawking said, "This is Magnus. We all have specialties around here. He's our computer guru."

Celeste held out a hand. "Nice to meet you."

Magnus took her much smaller hand in his. "You, too, Little girl."

She gasped. How did he know she was Little? She lifted her gaze to Hawking, wondering if he'd told all of his team. The thought embarrassed her.

Sadie wiggled free of her Daddy, Rocco, and came skipping toward them. "Don't worry, Celeste. These men may all look fierce and growly, but they are also all Daddies at heart."

"Hey..." Rocco growled. "Who's growly?" He was the only man she'd formally met so far because he'd brought Sadie to her room on the fourth floor earlier in the day.

Sadie giggled and rolled her eyes. "You are, Daddy."

He snickered as he pulled her back against his front and kissed the top of her head. He clearly adored her, and Celeste was jealous of their relationship.

Was it possible she could have something like that with Hawking? He seemed to think so. Heck, Hawking seemed certain she was his.

The other three hunks in the room introduced themselves one at a time. She hoped she would remember their names. *Kestrel, Phoenix, and Caesar.* She tried to commit them to memory.

Magnus spoke. "I went through your computer earlier. I suspect whoever your boss hired to find you used the IP address to track you down. Your phone, too."

"But I turned them both off," she argued, wrapping her arms around herself.

Magnus cringed. "I found a tracer on your computer that appears to download automatically when a device connects to the research facility server."

"Why are they always a step ahead of me?" she asked.

"Bad guys," Magnus answered pointedly.

Hawking set his hands on her shoulders. "It's okay now, Celeste. You're safe."

She gasped as a thought came to her. "But they know where I am, and they'll come back and try to get me and put you all in danger. I should go somewhere else and—"

Hawking wrapped his arms all the way around her and

pulled her back against his chest. "Shh," he whispered in her ear. "You're not going anywhere, and you're safe here."

Sadie groaned. "Yeah. Don't even try to talk these guys into letting you leave for their safety. Been there, done that. It's not going to happen."

Celeste turned to look at her new friend. "You were in danger?"

"Girl, three men tried to climb the side of a cliff, shooting at me. Lucky for me, these six oxen saved the day."

Celeste gasped, staring in shock at Sadie. "Someone shot at you? Why?"

"I might have sort of taken some data I wasn't supposed to have from my work that proved my boss was a very bad man, and he wanted me dead."

Celeste's knees went weak. She jerked her head around to look at Hawking. "That's kinda what I did."

Rocco cleared his throat. "I don't think you're helping Celeste feel better, Cookie," he said to Sadie. "Maybe keep the details to yourself for now."

Sadie cringed. "Sorry, Daddy. Sorry, Celeste."

Caesar cleared his throat. "This place is a lot safer than it was when we first arrived, Celeste. We have it fortified from every angle."

Hawking groaned. "And yet, a woman walked right into the resort today, grabbed a uniform and a cart, and pretended to be on staff. She even went to Celeste's room and got her to open the door."

Phoenix scowled. "You're right. I don't like it. I'm glad she ended up being harmless, but I also don't know how we can lock down any better than we already have. We don't want to alarm the guests. This resort will end up closing in a week if people find out they could be in the crosshairs of gunfire. Guns aren't even legal in New Zealand."

Kestrel nodded. "I agree. It's not like we can put up metal detectors at the gates, check every car for weapons, or question every person who comes to visit as if they're being grilled by the CIA. No one would come."

Celeste stood on wobbly feet, worry eating at her. "See? It's not safe for the guests. I should go somewhere else." She pointed at her laptop on Magnus's desk. "If I take that with me, they'll track me away from here and not endanger the guests."

Hawking made a strange noise and stiffened. "She has a good idea."

"You can't be serious," Sadie shouted, throwing her arms in the air. "You can't just let her leave. Have you all lost your minds?" She jerked her gaze around from one man to the next.

Rocco grabbed her around the waist and lifted her clear off the floor. "Sadie, sweetheart, stop."

"But, Daddy..."

Hawking tightened his grip on Celeste. "My Little girl isn't going anywhere. That's not what I mean. But we could take her phone and the computer somewhere else, or at least the trackable components."

Celeste finally understood what his intention was. "That might work," she murmured. "Everything on my computer is also on that external hard drive."

Magnus nodded. "Did you have that backed up, too, Little girl?"

She smirked and rolled her eyes. "Of course. I have two clouds."

"Good girl," Magnus said. "I made several copies too." He actually smiled at her proudly, and she was pretty sure he didn't smile often.

Hawking kissed her neck. "Smart woman."

She shivered at the touch of his lips. She kind of wished no one else was in the room and she could turn and kiss him properly. Based on the low groan coming from his lips, she guessed he felt the same way.

Rocco clapped his hands together. "Let's eat. We can meet in the morning to come up with a plan for relocating Celeste's computer. In the meantime, it stays off, and she works on a spare computer without interacting with the company's server."

Everyone nodded their agreement, and Hawking slipped his hand over Celeste's to guide her to the enormous table in the great room.

"Wow. This basement is amazing," she said in wonder as she looked around. The entertainment center was huge. So was the sectional in front of it. Most of them could easily sit around the giant-screen television and watch a movie.

She must have been lingering and drooling over the idea because Sadie leaned close to her and said, "They have all the cool animated movies, too. Maybe we can watch one after dinner."

"Or," Rocco interrupted, "maybe you'll be in bed early with a sore bottom for eating gummy bears without permission."

Celeste sucked in a breath and held it, her face heating with worry that Sadie would be mad at her for tattling. She had no experience in this department.

But Sadie didn't look at her at all. She thrust out her bottom lip and pouted. "Daddy, how did you find out?"

Rocco chuckled. "The wrappers were still in your pockets when I changed your clothes, Cookie." He cupped her face and kissed her like he didn't mind a bit that she'd been naughty.

He'd changed her clothes for her? Celeste stared at them

in awe, just now realizing that Sadie was no longer dressed in the professional attire she'd been wearing during the workday. She had on a comfortable outfit of leggings and a T-shirt. The T-shirt read, *I'm naughty, and I know it.*

Celeste had to cover her mouth to stifle a giggle.

"What's so funny, CB?" Hawking whispered in her ear as he guided her closer to the big table.

"Sadie's shirt," she whispered in return.

He chuckled. "Did you look at any clothes while you were *not* shopping this afternoon?"

She shrugged. "Maybe." She had, but she hadn't put them in the cart either. There was no way she could afford any of that. It had been a frivolous few hours during which she'd left her head and pretended she didn't have a monstrous problem looming over her. She'd also left her senses and pretended money was no object, and she could outfit a playroom for a queen as though it could be plucked from trees.

Celeste had made good money as a research scientist. She had an advanced degree and amazing qualifications. She'd lived frugally and had put most of her money in savings. But she didn't have access to that money right now, and she wouldn't dare use her credit cards, so that meant she would be relying on cash until it ran out. No way could she buy cute T-shirts, nor would she let Hawking purchase things for her.

"Oh," Sadie exclaimed as they all took their seats. She jumped down from her chair, rushed across the room, and pulled an envelope out of her purse. Seconds later, she returned and handed it to Celeste. "Mr. Kingsley said to give you this."

Celeste stared at the envelope, wondering what it could be. When she opened it, she gasped. It was the thousand dollars she'd left with Sadie to prepay for her stay at Danger Bluff. "Why are you giving me this?"

Sadie shrugged. "I was only holding it for you so you wouldn't panic when you first arrived."

Celeste's eyes went wide as she looked around the room. "You all already knew my problems before I got here?"

Hawking rubbed her back. "We did, CB. Mr. Kingsley is a powerful man, and he uses his immense wealth to help those in need who are deserving of his kindness."

Celeste felt tears welling up in her eyes. "Like he did earlier today for that woman and her son."

Hawking nodded. "Yes."

"How did he even know I was in trouble?" she murmured, mostly to herself.

Hawking leaned closer and kissed her cheek. "I doubt any of us will ever know or understand how Kingsley knows anything. We just have to accept it and do our part to help make the world a better place."

"One Little girl at a time, apparently," Sadie said jokingly.

Celeste was startled at her suggestion. She had a point. "Is that how you met Rocco?"

"Yep. He was assigned to protect me. He knew immediately he was my Daddy." She leaned over from her chair and wrapped her arms around his neck.

Celeste turned to look at Hawking. "Like you did," she said, stunned.

He shrugged. "We're starting to wonder if Kingsley has some kind of psychic matchmaking skills."

"When will I meet him?" Celeste asked.

"We're all wondering that, CB. None of us have met him. We don't even know where he is."

Her jaw dropped open as she looked around the table. "How did you all end up here in the first place then?"

Rocco answered her. "We were all saved by Kingsley at

some point in our lives, and we owed him a marker. He called us all together here a few weeks ago to start collecting our debt essentially."

Caesar chuckled. "Not that it's a hardship, mind you. We quickly fell in love with this place. The truth is that once we've each finished our assignments, we are free to go, no longer owing Kingsley, but we've agreed that we're a team. The six of us. None of us is going anywhere, certainly not until we've all finished our missions."

Celeste turned toward Hawking again. "Do I also owe Kingsley a marker for helping me out?"

He shook his head vehemently. "No, Little girl. Not you. Kingsley chose us because of our skills in order to assemble a power rescue team." He gave her hair a playful tug. "Though you are a magnificent scientist, I don't think he has any use for your skills when it comes to combat or surveillance. You won't owe Kingsley a thing. I promise."

"Speaking of which..." Magnus said, "I was digging around in your life and discovered you are quite accomplished. PhDs in both microbiology and chemistry. Amazing accolades from your university. Several published works. And, I'm no scientist, but I'm smart enough to know that the data you have on that computer would suggest you've discovered a treatment that will keep cancer cells from reproducing as rapidly as they do."

Everyone stared at Celeste.

She lowered her gaze, letting her hair fall across her cheeks to hide her embarrassment while she shrugged. "It's just a job."

"Celeste!" Sadie exclaimed. "That's not just a job."

Hawking tugged her chair closer to his and wrapped an arm around her. He pulled her cheek against his shoulder and kissed the top of her head. "You're an amazing woman, Celeste Blanke. I'm humbled to be your Daddy."

She bit her lip at his announcement to the entire room, though she suspected everyone already knew he'd claimed her as his Little girl. Hell, the truth was, he'd probably claimed her as his own before she'd ever met him. Out of everyone in the room, she'd been the last to know.

"We should eat before this food gets cold," Phoenix announced.

Celeste was grateful. She still felt a bit overwhelmed by all the attention.

The moment Phoenix took the lids off the steaming food in the middle of the table, the room filled with the amazing aroma of Mexican spices.

Celeste's mouth watered as she stared at the giant pans of enchiladas and burritos. There were also large bowls of refried beans and rice, as well as all the fixings.

"That smells so good," Hawking said as his stomach grumbled. He was the first to reach out and pull a pan of enchiladas toward them. "May I serve you, CB?"

"Yes, please, Daddy." She couldn't see any reason to hold back on calling him Daddy in front of everyone in this room. It felt good. It felt real. It felt like home. And Lord knew it had been a long time since Celeste had had a family to call her own.

Her own parents had both passed, and she had no siblings. She'd dedicated herself to science for as long as she could remember and hadn't taken this much time off from research in many years.

As the platters were passed around the table, she watched everyone laughing and chatting and felt so warm and fuzzy inside. Could this really be her life now? Hawking seemed to think so.

Chapter Ten

"Why does Hawking call you CB?" Sadie asked from across the table as they all finished stuffing themselves with the most delicious Mexican food.

She glanced at him, hoping he would field this question.

Hawking reached for her hand under the table and gave it a squeeze. "It's short for the nickname I gave her."

"Oh." Sadie sat up straighter. "Like my Daddy calls me Cookie."

"Yep."

"It's not very creative, Hawking," Kestrel taunted. "Celeste Blanke. CB. Couldn't you come up with something cuter, like honey, sweety, or baby?"

Celeste couldn't help the giggle that escaped. "That was an accident. It doesn't stand for Celeste Blanke."

Sadie grinned wide. "Is it a secret?"

Celeste felt her cheeks heat. Did she want all these people to know her Daddy called her Cuddle Bug? Then again, why should she care? It was his nickname. Not hers.

She didn't invent it. He should be the one to decide if it embarrassed him.

Hawking didn't even flinch. "It's simple. My Little girl is cute as a bug, and she likes to cuddle up against me at night. So, Cuddle Bug."

"That's so sweet." Sadie sighed as though she'd just heard the most romantic gesture.

"Celeste has only been here one night," Phoenix taunted.

Sadie was sitting next to him, and she reached over and swatted him on the shoulder. "Don't judge. Wait until you find your Little girl."

He chuckled good-naturedly.

"Time for dessert," Magnus said as he rose from the table and returned a moment later with something he'd pulled out of the fridge.

"Do we need to fill out surveys about taste palettes again?" Sadie asked, her voice teasing.

Magnus shot her a playful glare. "Flavor profiles, Little girl. They are an important part of the culinary experience. And yes. The chef has requested our input about the meal again tonight."

Celeste finally understood the joking, and she loved it. Apparently, Magnus was knowledgeable in the kitchen. Interesting. He was mostly quiet and all business. Now, it looked as though he was also a foodie.

"Is that some kind of mousse?" Caesar asked.

"I think it's flan," Magnus said.

"Flan?" Phoenix lifted a brow.

"Yes," Sadie said, nodding. "It's popular in Mexico, therefore a fitting end to the meal."

Soon, they were all devouring the most delicious custard dish Celeste had ever put in her mouth. She didn't know anything about flavor profiles or taste palettes, but she knew good food when she ate it, and she'd hit the food jackpot when she'd decided to hide out indefinitely at Danger Bluff Mountain Resort.

As she finished the last bite, she turned to look at her Daddy. Yeah, she'd definitely hit the jackpot.

"Everything okay?" Hawking asked. "Are you still hungry?"

"I'm chocka."

"Does that mean sick?" he asked in concern.

Her giggle seemed to reassure him. "No! Chocka means full. I think you in the U.S. say stuffed?"

His answering grin made it hard for her to remember that she was in danger. Dr. Hughes knew she'd taken the data. He knew she was well aware that someone in his office had altered it and lied as an excuse to fire her. She suspected the research facility where she worked had taken a kickback from at least one pharmaceutical company to put an end to her research. It didn't take the proverbial rocket scientist to figure out that if anyone found out about her treatment plan, big pharma would stand to lose a lot of money.

The entire thing made her sick to her stomach. Her life was probably in danger. She'd lost her job, and she had no idea if she would ever get another in her field. Everything was upside down and inside out.

However, the man next to her adored her and had pledged to take care of her in ways she'd never dreamed would happen to her.

She realized she was staring at him when he smiled, leaned closer, and said, "Let's go back to my apartment." His voice was deep and sexy.

Celeste clenched her legs together. The arousal she felt was stronger than anything she'd ever experienced. Would he make love to her tonight? He'd said she could sleep with him.

He'd even suggested he preferred it. But was he only saying that because he wanted her to be safe? Or did he want to have sex with her?

"Yes," she breathed out.

Hawking pushed up from the table. "I know we all have more questions for Celeste, but let's table it until tomorrow. My Little girl is exhausted."

Magnus rose and walked toward the elevators with them. "Celeste, can you come down in the morning and meet with me about what's on your computer so I'll understand better how high the stakes are?"

"Yes."

He stopped and adjusted the ballcap on his head. "The truth is, I'd feel better if you were down here with me during the day. Is that okay?" He glanced at Hawking.

Hawking blew out a long breath. "Yes. I'd feel better if she were down here, too. I don't think I could effectively do my job managing security if I didn't know she was protected."

Magnus gave a nod. "It's settled then. Bring Celeste down here before you leave in the morning. I'll have a computer set up for her and get her prints put in the system at that time, too."

Celeste felt like they were both being a bit high-handed, not even asking her how she felt about the sequestration. But she knew they were just worried about her safety. Plus, she was itching to open her files and do some more research. It had been days since she'd last put on her scientist's hat. She could use the stimulation and the distraction.

She realized both men were staring at her. "What?" she asked, glancing back and forth between them.

Hawking set a hand on her back. "Are you okay with that plan?"

She smiled. Ah, so they were finally going to include her.

"Yes, Daddy," she said in the sweetest voice. She felt like skipping to the elevator.

Two minutes later, they were in Daddy's apartment. He led her straight through to his bedroom. "Bath or shower, CB?"

She followed him into the huge master bath and stared longingly at the huge, jetted bathtub. Her mouth nearly watered. She hadn't had a bath in a long time. She'd never felt like she had enough time to luxuriate in a tub. The thought of soaking with bubbles all around her made her nearly drool.

Hawking chuckled. "I guess you'd like to take a bath." He put the stopper in the bottom, turned on the water, and adjusted it until he got it just right.

"I'd love it. Do you mind?"

"Nope. Do *you* mind if I join you?"

She gave him a slow smile while feeling kind of shocked by his suggestion. It was loaded with possibilities. But she wasn't sorry. She'd been panting after him from the moment she'd met him and had lusted harder with every kiss he'd given her.

Celeste didn't have a lot of experience with men, but she wasn't a virgin. She'd had sex with men sometimes—usually with other men in her field. None of them had impressed her. They'd mostly been awkward and sloppy. She hadn't found sex to be something she longed to participate in.

Until she'd met Hawking. With his dark skin and darker eyes, she'd found herself staring at him several times. Every time he'd held her hand or wrapped his arms around her, she'd been mesmerized by the difference in their skin tones. Mesmerized in the way that made her nipples hard and her pussy wet.

"Celeste?" Hawking prompted.

She shook herself out of her lusty thoughts. "What?"

He chuckled as he sauntered closer to her. He set his hands on her hips and met her gaze. "I asked if you'd like me to join you. You didn't answer, but you did look ready to rip my clothes off. Is that a yes?"

"Are you going to make love to me?" she blurted.

"Are you ready for that step in our relationship? I don't want you to feel pressured. I can take a bath with you without having sex, CB."

She licked her lips and decided to be brave. "I think I'd like you to have sex with me."

He gave her a slow smile. "You think?" he teased.

"I know I would. And then I'd like you to sleep under the covers this time so I can truly snuggle up with you like your cuddle bug."

"I'd really like that, Celeste." He grabbed the hem of her shirt and drew it over her head before holding her biceps and staring at her bra-covered chest. "Damn. You are so beautiful. I saw a picture of you dressed in the sexiest emerald dress before you got here. It was stunning, but it didn't do you justice."

She blushed. "You saw a picture from the gala?"

"Uh-huh. It was in the information Kingsley gave me when he assigned me to protect you. You were so gorgeous that I had to beat the rest of the team back with a stick to get them to stop staring at you."

Celeste gasped. "Everyone saw that picture? I know the one. It was in the tabloids."

"Yep. Does that embarrass you? It shouldn't. It wasn't indecent. It was just so stunning that I got possessive."

She giggled. "You hadn't met me."

"I didn't need to, CB. I just knew."

"Well, I hate to bust your bubble, but I don't usually look

like that. I never wear makeup. I don't even know how to put it on. I'm a science nerd through and through. A hairdresser and a makeup artist worked their magic on me for that event."

He lowered his lips and kissed her neck before trailing nibbling kisses between the cups of her bra. "Little girl, I do not need makeup or fancy hair. You are the most delightful, beautiful, intelligent, sexy woman I've ever met. I'm in awe of everything about you. Hell, after Magnus's announcement about your multiple advanced degrees, I'm feeling a bit humbled and unworthy."

It was hard to focus on his words while he continued to kiss her cleavage. But she caught that last part clearly and leaned back. "Don't be ridiculous." She was panting, but she tried to continue to focus. "You are so much more interesting than me. Muscular and worldly and knowledgeable and savvy. I only know about science things."

He slid his hands up her back and lifted his face to meet her gaze. "That's not true. You have a tremendous amount of common sense, Celeste. You had everything in place for any eventuality. You had cash on hand. You knew to turn off your phone and computer. You knew not to stay in your apartment for another minute. You made wise decisions that kept you alive, and I'm so fucking glad."

As soon as he finished speaking, he popped the clasp on her bra. As it slid down her arms, she shivered.

His gaze was heated and lustful as he took in her rounded breasts. She knew she was an anomaly. Dressed in her usual baggy clothing, she looked fit and toned. Only when she wore something fitted perfectly or was nude did her curves reveal themselves. She'd never even attempted to look like one of those slender cover models. Celeste ran to release the tension of the day and to have dedicated thinking time—not because she wanted to be sexier. To her delight, the look on Hawking's face told her he was definitely not disappointed.

"Celeste..." The word was soft and breathy, and wetness gathered between her legs. Her Daddy certainly knew how to make her feel like a princess.

He lowered his lips to one of her nipples and kissed it reverently, making her breath hitch. The way he worshipped her was so sweet and endearing that emotion welled up inside her. "Hawking..."

The sound of his name on her lips startled her. It didn't sound anything like her. She'd been calling him Daddy for the past few hours, but she wanted to use his real name while he touched her so intimately.

He was still fully clothed, and she had on her pants, but all she could do was hold on to his biceps as he switched back and forth between her breasts, lavishing them with his lips and tongue.

She'd never been this aroused before. Not alone with her vibrator, and certainly not with any previous man.

When he released her nipple and lifted his gaze, he was panting and grinning. "Fuck, but you are sexy and so responsive. Are you wet for me, CB?"

She nodded, her face heating. While she had marginal control over at least a few brain cells, she grabbed the hem of his shirt and pulled it up.

He helped her tug it over his head before his fingers came to the button on her jeans.

She matched him, holding his gaze while she tackled his button. She wanted to see him. Hell, she wanted to do far more than see him. She had the oddest urge to drop onto her knees and take him into her mouth.

She'd never given a blow job before. She'd never even

considered it. But with Hawking, she felt strange new carnal urges.

They simultaneously shoved each other's jeans over hips and down thighs before she realized they both had on shoes and were about to be comically stuck.

"Little girl, wait for Daddy." Hawking took a step back and ripped off the rest of his clothes. Pausing, he let her look over his body.

Her gaze roamed all over his delectable body, taking in his short, tidy haircut and beard, the array of tattoos, his chiseled muscles, and the V of his stomach that led to the most impressive cock she'd ever set eyes on.

Thank God I'm not a virgin. Though it had been a long time since she'd had sex. He was going to stretch her.

Hawking's hands were fisted at his sides as if he were struggling to hold back.

When she raised her gaze to meet his, she pleaded, "Me, now."

Suddenly, he broke the silence. "Now, I get to finish unwrapping my present."

Kneeling at her feet, Hawking pressed a kiss just above the line of her brief panties. Off-balanced by her need, Celeste steadied herself by clinging to his broad shoulders. She stepped when directed as he stripped off her shoes and the last of her clothing.

"Bath, naughty girl." He stood and pointed toward the tub.

Chapter Eleven

Hawking had no idea how he was going to survive this bathing session without impaling his fucking sexy Little girl while they were still in the tub. His cock was rock hard.

Actually, sexy didn't accurately describe Celeste. He'd seen the pictures. He'd known she was beautifully shaped under that lab coat. The photo of her in that damn green dress had made every man on his team lean in to get a closer look.

But this...naked Celeste... This was going to bring him to his knees. Her skin was so soft and smooth. Her nipples were the loveliest shade of pink—puckered and begging for attention.

He'd noticed while he'd been worshipping them that she liked it when he kissed the undersides of her breasts or stroked his thumbs along the soft, full globes.

Breaking the spell, he turned toward the tub and climbed in first before reaching for his Little girl's hand to help her over the side. When she hesitated, he turned the water off and lowered himself, spreading his legs. "Sit here, CB."

She pulled the band from the back of her hair, twisted the entire length around on top of her head, and replaced the band to keep it out of the water.

Watching her do this was mesmerizing. With her arms lifted in the air and his view from below her, he found it hard to breathe. Her breasts were spectacular, and even sexier lifted high like that.

Finally, she followed his instructions, lowering her body to sit nestled between his legs so that her back was to his front. She was slightly stiff and trembling.

He wasn't sure how much experience she had with sex. If it was minimal, that might explain the nerves coming out. She was a grown woman, though. Thirty-two years old. Only three years younger than him.

Hawking gently wrapped an arm around her middle and silently encouraged her to lean back into him. Her waist was tiny, and he easily enveloped her, loving the way her breasts rested against his forearm.

Setting his lips against her ear, he whispered, "Relax, Cuddle Bug. You're very tense. Nothing is going to happen between us that you aren't ready for."

"I'm ready," she whispered. "I'm just nervous. It's..."

"It's what, CB?" He trailed his fingers along her thigh under the water.

"It's been a long time, and I'm not very worldly about sex either. I've never been with anyone who, uh..."

He smiled. He liked her words. "Who what?" he encouraged as he let his fingers inch between her legs.

She blew out an exasperated breath as if this was a very difficult conversation.

Hawking nudged her legs wider and stroked his fingers along her labia.

Celeste grabbed his thighs with both hands and whimpered.

He whispered into her ear again. "Tell me what you were going to say, Celeste."

She gasped and stiffened as he eased a finger into her channel. Damn, she was tight.

"You've never been with anyone who what, CB?" he repeated. He really wanted to hear what she had to say.

Her breathing was labored as she leaned her head back against his shoulder. "Who made me feel like this," she murmured. "Who made me...come."

The last word was so soft he almost didn't hear it, but he got it. And his dick did too. "You haven't had very good lovers then, CB." He added a second finger to her tight sheath and pressed his thumb against her clit.

Her response was nothing more than a whimper. She probably had no idea she was writhing in his grip. Good thing he had an arm around her waist to steady her. Otherwise, she might have shot out of the tub when he touched her clit.

"*Oh,*" she exclaimed. "I can't... I mean, I don't... Oh God..."

He was fist-pumping in his head, but he managed to keep his arm steady around her waist while stroking her breast at the same time.

When he pinched her nipple, she cried out. "Hawking!"

He could sense her at war in her head. "Let it feel good, Cuddle Bug. Don't fight it."

"But..." She gasped several times. She was so delightful. "Vibrator..."

"Mmm. I don't think we need a vibrator, Little girl." He tried not to chuckle. He rubbed her clit while he tugged on her nipple.

Celeste screamed as her entire body convulsed in his

arms. It was the most beautiful experience of his life. So raw and natural.

He kissed her neck as he eased his fingers out of her pussy. "You're amazing, Celeste. Stunning."

She was breathing heavily. "Oh my God. You..." She finally relaxed completely against him, her body going limp.

With her head on his shoulder, he could see her lick her lips. "I've never had an orgasm without a vibrator," she told him.

"I figured that. And do you have a vibrator with you here in our apartment?" He really wanted to know.

She shook her head. "No. It..." Her cheeks turned bright pink as she pursed her lips.

"It what?" he asked in confusion.

She sighed, seemingly resigned to answering him. "When I got to my apartment and found it ransacked, my vibrator was turned on and tossed on my bed. It was humiliating. I turned it off and dropped it in the trash."

Hawking flinched at her revelation. What sort of weird fucker would do something like that just to taunt her while he searched for information? What an asshole.

"That was honestly the worst part about the break-in. It felt like I'd been violated in a weird way."

"Understandable. So, you haven't had an orgasm in several days." No wonder she was so sensitive.

She turned her head and stared at him before rolling her eyes. "It's been quite a bit longer than that. I've been busy at work for months. All I've managed to do when I wasn't at the lab was drop into bed and sleep. Masturbation wasn't high on my priority list."

He smiled and kissed her nose. "Then we need to make up for lost time."

She stared at him with wide eyes. "Uhhh, that was probably a fluke."

He chuckled. "That was *not* a fluke, Cuddle Bug. That was your body responding to your Daddy's touch. It's going to happen a lot." He picked up the bar of soap from the ledge along the side of the tub and ran it up and down her arms, letting her think.

Celeste mewled contentedly while he washed her. She even spread her legs for him and let him clean her intimately, not saying a word when he lingered.

He leaned her forward so he could wash himself, and then he released the water and lifted her out of the tub to set her on her feet.

When she shivered from the cool air in the room, he quickly grabbed a huge fluffy towel and wrapped it around her. "Better?"

"Yes, Daddy," she said in the sweetest Little voice.

After drying himself, he guided her to the sink, put toothpaste on both their toothbrushes, and set hers in her hand.

She seemed happy and more relaxed now that she'd had an orgasm. He looked forward to making her look that way often.

"Your turn," she said as she put her toothbrush in the holder next to his and lowered her gaze to the bulge in his towel.

He smirked, assuming she was referring to his rigid cock currently tenting the towel around his waist. "My turn?" He removed his towel and hung it on the rack before tugging hers off and doing the same.

"Yep." She turned on her feet and trotted into the master bedroom.

Hawking drew a deep breath and let it out slowly as he

followed her. He hated to let her down, but things weren't going to go quite how she envisioned.

When she reached the bed, she pulled the comforter and sheet back and sat on the edge. It was obvious she was trying to exude confidence and power, but she was trembling with nerves, and he was equally certain she'd never been in a situation like this or had ever suggested she'd take care of a man.

He cupped her face and leaned in to kiss her, not pulling back until she was shaking and kiss-drunk. When he did finally release her swollen lips, she stared at him.

"Here's what's going to happen, Cuddle Bug. First, I'm going to turn you over and give you your first spanking because I know you're curious. Then, I'm going to spread your legs open and eat your pretty pussy until you come so hard your eyes roll back. And if you're not too sated, I'll make sweet love to you."

Her eyes widened. "But I already came, and you..."

He chuckled and shook his head. "There will never be a scorecard, CB. Daddy will always make sure you come first and usually more than once."

She licked her precious lips. "I'm not going to come... again, Daddy," she whispered.

He gave her a quick kiss. "If you don't, that's fine. Let's start with the spanking." He tapped her hips and nodded toward the head of the bed. "On your tummy. Lie close to the edge so I can reach you."

She hesitated. "What if I don't like it, Daddy?"

"I'm going to start nice and slow and check in with you often. If by some chance you hate being spanked, we'll come up with other forms of punishment for when you misbehave."

She gaped at him. "I don't misbehave."

He chuckled. "Is that so?"

"Never. The first time I ever even broke a rule was when

I used a co-worker's login after I'd been terminated to copy data proving my research wasn't flawed."

"I bet when you're in your Little headspace, you'll get into trouble, CB. I can already tell that Sadie is itching to drag you down with her in planned shenanigans."

"You mean like the gummy bear incident?"

"Yep. I'm sure she has a long list of possibilities."

"Why would she do that? I don't understand why anyone would want their bottom spanked."

"You will in a minute, CB. Now turn over and stop stalling."

She sighed as she rolled onto her tummy, tucking her arms in next to her breasts.

Hawking grabbed a pillow. "Lift your hips for me, Cuddle Bug."

She turned her head toward him and did as he asked, biting her lip when he tucked the pillow under her tummy. "There. Spread your legs. I don't want you to squeeze your thighs together while I'm spanking you."

Her breath hitched as she parted her knees.

"Good girl." He rubbed her bottom. Damn, her derriere was fine. He could squeeze and look at it all night. But he had a mission.

"It's going to hurt," she murmured.

"Nope. Not at first. The key is to build up the pressure gradually. You'll see." He set one hand on the small of her back just in case she jumped, lifted his hand from her bottom, and swatted her left cheek.

She flinched.

He did it again on the right side, not hard enough to even sting. Leaning over to her ear, he whispered, "Did that hurt?"

"No, Daddy."

"See?"

"Well, the jury is still out." She squirmed under his palm.

He chuckled. "But you're curious and ready for more, aren't you?"

"I guess." She shrugged as if she didn't care one way or the other.

Hawking gave her another half a dozen swats, peppering both sides with barely enough pressure to have an impact. When she drew her knees together, he stopped and tapped her thighs. "Legs parted, Celeste," he said, deepening his voice.

A soft moan escaped her lips. She liked this. He would bet money her pussy was wet.

"Good girl." He resumed spanking her, making sure to cover all her bottom and the upper swell of her thighs.

The next time he stopped to check in with her, she was panting.

"Good?"

"Yes, Sir," she whispered. Did she know she lifted her cute bottom to get better contact with his palm?

"More?"

"I guess."

He had to work hard not to chuckle at her nonchalance as he spanked her a bit harder. Her bottom was turning a nice shade of pink when she started moaning and squirming.

Hawking decided to put her out of her misery and give her the full package. After four more swats, each one harder than the last, he reached between her legs, dragged his fingers through her dripping wet folds, and thrust two of them into her warmth.

Celeste cried out, lifting her head and wiggling as much as she could with his palm holding her down. "Daddy!"

He found her clit next and rubbed it until she stopped breathing altogether. One more stroke over her clit sent her into the stratosphere. Her body seemed to levitate off the bed as she milked his fingers and pulsed against him.

Before the orgasm had a chance to fully die down, Hawking removed his fingers, grabbed her hips, and flipped her onto her back. She was like a rag doll as he maneuvered her so her ass was on the edge of the mattress, her feet hanging off the sides.

Her head was lolling back and forth, her eyes open but seeing nothing.

Hawking grabbed her knees, bent her legs, and pushed them wide apart above her hips. In the next moment, he lowered his mouth to the most precious pussy on earth, dragged his tongue up through her folds, and flicked it over her clit.

Celeste arched her back off the bed as she grabbed for his shoulders. Speechless.

He sucked her clit into his mouth and circled it with his tongue until she was writhing so violently it was hard to hold her steady.

Her hands gripped his shoulders, but her feeble attempts to dislodge him were no match for his determination to give her one more orgasm.

She needed to know. She needed to understand that she could and would be able to come for him without toys. It was an appropriate follow-up to the lesson she'd just received. She could and would enjoy getting her bottom spanked.

"Hawking!" she shouted as she bucked and squirmed. "Oh God."

He thrust his tongue into her before laving her clit again and then tormenting it with rapid flicks.

Celeste lifted her hips clear off the mattress as she came a third time.

He helped her ride the waves, gradually easing back on

the sucks and licks until she began to settle. Finally, he lifted his lips, wiped his mouth on the sheet, and met her gaze.

She was definitely sex-drunk. She had that glassy look he'd been aiming for, the one that said he could spank her and suck her pussy anytime he wanted.

"Are Daddies always right?" she murmured.

"Nope. We do make mistakes, but I expect you to trust me to know your limits and give me the benefit of the doubt that I can take you to new heights."

"Okay, Daddy." She lifted her arms and wrapped them around his neck. "Will you please make love to me now?"

"I'd love to, Cuddle Bug." He grabbed her hips and scooted her to the middle of the bed before yanking open the drawer on his nightstand to retrieve a condom. Suited up, he crawled between her legs and hovered over her.

She smiled at him from hooded eyes and boldly wrapped her ankles around his waist. "You're very big, Daddy."

He chuckled. "Too big, you think? Should we wait to have sex another day so I can stretch you out some more first?"

She shook her head. "No. I need you now. Don't tease me anymore, Daddy."

Hawking nestled himself at her entrance, watching her face as he slowly glided into her warmth. He wanted to take it slow this first time. The stretch was going to be tight. But it was damn difficult to control himself. His cock had been beyond hard for hours. It wanted the world, and it wanted it now.

"More, Daddy," she encouraged, lifting her hips to meet him.

"Okay, CB." He was about halfway inside her when he pulled out and slammed back in to the hilt.

She didn't wince. In fact, she sighed contentedly and

held on to him with her ankles. Her hands ran up and down his back and butt cheeks. "Yes," she purred. "Do it again."

There was no way to deny her or himself. Hawking set up a rhythm, barely able to hold back his own orgasm. He wasn't going to last long this first time, though, and there was no fighting it. In no time, his balls drew up, and his cock swelled further.

Wanting to take his Little girl over the edge one more time with him, he reached between their bodies, found her clit with his middle finger, and rubbed it hard. In seconds, she screamed. A second later, he joined her. Heaven.

Chapter Twelve

Celeste woke up smiling, though she wasn't sure why at first. She blinked her eyes several times before she remembered where she was and what she'd done last night.

The bed was empty next to her, but she could hear the shower running in the bathroom. The door was ajar, too. Her Daddy hadn't even shut or locked the door.

She winced as she tried to sit up. Her entire body felt deliciously sore from... *Oh. My. God...* Four orgasms. *Four.* She hadn't expected to ever orgasm with a man. She'd been startled when he'd managed to do it the first time but wrote it off as a fluke in her head, probably caused by pent-up sexual frustration.

But that wouldn't explain the second, third, and fourth orgasms. Her eyeballs rolled up in their sockets as she remembered that last one. She certainly had never expected to come during sex. Hawking had seemed to anticipate what she'd needed. Goodness knows, he'd lavished her with perfectly-timed, intimate caresses.

Giggling, she shoved her way off the bed and padded

toward the bathroom. She needed to see him. Touch him. Verify he was real.

When she stepped inside, he spotted her and smiled. "Hey, Little girl. I didn't mean to wake you."

She came to him, feeling bold, and opened the shower door to step inside.

He grinned broadly and pulled her under the water before kissing her all over her face, neck, and shoulders until she laughed.

"You're really here," she said when he finally stopped.

"Where else would I be?"

"In an alternate dimension I conjured up in my mind to fulfill my Daddy needs."

He chuckled. "Nope. We're both in the same dimension, and I'll happily fulfill your Daddy needs for the rest of your life."

She ran her hands up and down his chest, admiring the artwork and the way her skin looked against his. It was so erotic. "That's a long time."

"Not long enough." He grabbed the soap and went to work washing her body, massaging her in all the right places until she was putty.

"You're so good at that. Is there anything you're not good at?"

"We'll see in a few hours."

When she looked at him, his eyes were dancing. "What happens in a few hours?"

"You'll find out soon enough." He angled her head under the water to wet her hair and then grabbed the shampoo.

When she lowered her gaze to his erection, he lifted her chin. "No time for that, Little girl. Daddy has to get to work, so you need to be dressed and ready to go downstairs in about twenty minutes."

His reminder made her sober. "I don't like thinking about you possibly confronting bad guys."

He gave her a quick peck after rinsing her hair. "I'll be fine. I'm good at finding bad guys and protecting Little girls."

After ushering her out of the shower, he dried her body and took her hand. "Clothes, hair, teeth, ten minutes, CB." He patted her bottom, angling her toward the closet.

"When did you hang up my clothes in here?" she asked as she stared at the hangers on one side of the large closet. She didn't have much, but it was all here. Her suitcase was also stowed on the shelf above everything.

"I've been up for two hours, Cuddle Bug."

She twisted around, shocked. "Two hours?"

"Yep." He was already sitting on the edge of the bed, fully dressed, putting on his shoes.

She was still dumbfounded and naked. "Maybe I could just go downstairs as soon as I'm ready so I'm not holding you up," she suggested. She'd only be a few minutes behind him.

He shook his head as he headed for the dresser. "Nope. For one thing, you don't have access to the basement yet. Magnus needs to register your prints in the system so the elevators will open for you on that lower floor."

He came toward her with a pair of panties and handed them to her. "Do you want to dress yourself, or would you like Daddy to do it?"

She took the panties from him and put them on. "I can do it," she murmured.

He handed her a bra next, still talking. "You can order whatever you want for breakfast from the kitchen, and they'll bring it down." He grabbed a pair of her jeans and tossed them to her. "I'll come get you for lunch so we can come back up here. By then, your surprise will have arrived."

"Surprise?" Her mind was whirling as he pulled a shirt over her head and handed her a pair of tennis shoes.

Without waiting for her to put them on, he guided her back into the bathroom, grabbed her brush, and combed out her damp hair.

She stared in awe at their reflection in the mirror as he parted her hair and deftly fixed two low pigtails at the back of her head.

When he tried to brush her teeth for her, she snagged the toothbrush from his hand and did it herself while he chuckled.

"Shoes, Little girl."

She followed him to the bedroom again, sat on the bed, and put them on. When had he made the bed? While she'd brushed her teeth?

"Ready?"

She felt like she'd run a marathon and had whiplash at the same time. He'd done most of the work getting her ready. She looked around, trying to think if she needed anything, but everything she could need this morning was already in the basement except for her new phone, which Daddy set in her palm on their way to the door.

"You're a taskmaster in the morning," she murmured.

"Yep." He set a hand on the small of her back and led her to the elevator.

"What is this surprise you have coming for me?" she asked, still trying to get her bearings.

"You'll see. It wouldn't be a surprise if I told you, would it?"

She looked up at him when he threaded their fingers together and brought her knuckles to his lips. "But the surprise will prove whether you're good at everything?" she asked, remembering his words.

"Well, maybe not *everything*. But it will prove if I'm good at one more thing." He guided her off the elevator and into the basement control center.

Magnus was already seated at the wide expanse of monitors. "Hey there, Little girl." He rose from his seat and adjusted his ball cap. "Did you have breakfast yet?"

Hawking answered for her. "She didn't. She's apparently not a morning person," he teased. "I bet she'll be ready to order something soon." He grabbed her chin, kissed her soundly, and grinned. "See you in a few hours."

And then he was gone, and Celeste felt like the air left the room with him.

She still stared at the closed elevator doors while Magnus spoke behind her. "I figure after breakfast, we can get you set up to do your research from here. It looks pretty important. I bet you have no intention of stopping it just because the company you worked for took a bribe."

She turned to face him and drew a deep breath. "You're right. I know it's not exactly legal. The research belongs to the facility where I worked. Just because the discovery and all the work is mine doesn't mean I get to continue doing it." She admitted. Magnus seemed like the sort of man who would understand what she was talking about.

He nodded. "It looks like damn important research, Little girl. I don't blame you. Hopefully, in the end, you'll be able to legally get back into it."

She blew out a breath and let her shoulders relax. He understood. "Do you think I can work from down here?"

"Yep. This isn't a lab, of course. I can't really turn this into a biology lab, but I would bet that's not what you need in the short term anyway."

"No. I need to pull together all the information into a neat, tidy package. It's all raw data now," she admitted.

"Then, is there a review or publication process?"

"Usually, the company you work for handles all of that. For something this big, it would be handled with incredible secrecy to make sure no one steals your work."

"It's just you for now, Celeste. What should your first step be?" Magnus seemed to be coaching her through the process of setting up the steps to reveal the discovery to the world.

"I need to organize my data and get in touch with other companies and agencies around the world until I find one that will listen."

She stood there, staring at him. In less than thirty seconds, Magnus had planted ideas in her head that she hadn't even considered. She'd been thinking about nothing but staying alive for days. However, he was right. She needed to get back to work. There were cancer patients who needed her in their court.

Chapter Thirteen

"Hey there, Cuddle Bug."

Celeste spun in her new swivel chair at the sound of Hawking's voice. "What are you doing here?" she asked as she pushed off the chair and rushed to jump into his arms.

He chuckled. "It's lunchtime. I came to get you so we can go upstairs where your surprise is."

"Already?" She'd been so focused she hadn't even noticed the passage of time.

Magnus came up beside them. "You have to stay on top of this one," he told Daddy with a smirk.

"Yeah?"

"Yep. When she gets into her research, she tunes out the planet. If I hadn't told her to stop and eat breakfast, she wouldn't have realized she was starving. I even sent her to the potty twice."

Embarrassed, Celeste buried her face in her Daddy's shoulder. Magnus was correct. He'd described her perfectly.

"That doesn't surprise me. Thanks for the warning and

for keeping an eye on this Little girl this morning." Hawking hefted her up higher around his waist.

"My pleasure. She's a genius. It's a joy to watch her work." He waved over his shoulder as he returned to his station.

Celeste lifted her head as they entered the elevator. "What's the surprise, Daddy?"

"You'll see."

As soon as they entered the apartment, he let her slide down his body and turned her around to face the small living room.

Celeste gasped. It was littered with so many things. Things for her playroom. Things she'd looked at yesterday online but hadn't put in the cart to check out.

She took a step forward and touched the closest thing—a clear bag with bedding for the daybed. Exactly the one she'd lusted after. "How did you do this, Daddy? I didn't put it in the cart."

"Ahhh, but you did look at it. All I had to do was go through your recently searched list for each store." He winked at her.

Her jaw fell open, her mind spinning. She hadn't thought of that. "But when?"

"After you fell asleep last night, I opened my laptop, placed all the orders, and sent someone to pick everything up this morning." He wrapped his arms around her and kissed her. "Good surprise?"

"The best. But I don't like you spending this much money on me, Daddy."

"You're going to have to get over that, Cuddle Bug. If I want to spoil you, I will. There are also a few things in here I need to take care of you."

"Like what?"

He reached into the pile and pulled out a smallish box. Opening it up, he pulled out a sparkly green water bottle. "I would bet that you don't drink enough water for a lot of reasons. You don't want to stop to go to the bathroom. You can't have an open container to possibly spill something over your computer or your work. You probably don't like the taste of water."

Hawking chuckled at the look of shock on her face. "So that's a triple confirmation. You need to stay hydrated to keep your brain operating at full speed. Check this one out."

Handing her the gorgeous bottle, he watched as she turned it around.

"It has CB on it!"

"It does. Look at the lid," Hawking directed.

Celeste flipped open the transparent top that had a hinge on one side so it wouldn't get lost. A flexible straw popped up as the lid moved. She closed it and watched the drinking tube disappear.

"You can't spill it and you can easily get a drink. The straw will help you drink more water. There's one more feature."

"What? It turns water into a soft drink?" she asked, sarcastically.

"No. Even better." As he expected, her curiosity prompted her to unscrew the top as he pantomimed the gesture.

"Is this one of those fruit things?" she asked, staring into the bottle.

"Yes. Want to try it out?"

"Definitely, but it can wait. I want to see all this stuff."

"You'll have to wait until Daddy gets off tonight. Then

you can decide if you want to go for a run before dinner or unpack some of the goodies."

"That's not fair. I want to do both of those things."

He watched her expression and knew she was struggling not to rebel. "I promise we'll eventually get all the pretties out so you can see them."

She sighed. "Okay. Can I take my new water bottle?" She held it so tightly he could see her knuckles were turning white.

"Definitely. Let's wash it and fill it up. Do you want to put some fruit in there?"

"Yes. Strawberries."

"That does sound good. Let's go." Hawking took her other hand and led her out of the package-filled room. Quickly, they filled the water bottle, and Hawking called the kitchen to have them leave strawberries and kiwis at the front desk for him to pick up.

Within a few minutes, they were seated at the table in the basement munching on sandwiches and veggies the kitchen had prepared for them.

Celeste took a tentative drink from her new water bottle. "That's really good."

"Told ya." Hawking nudged her with his elbow. "You should listen to Daddy. I know things."

"That's it!" Celeste stood and ran to her computer.

Hawking watched her type furiously on the keys before looking over at Magnus who had noted Celeste's actions as well. When the computer guy looked at him and shook his head slightly, it confirmed what Hawking already knew. She was on a roll with something, and he wouldn't interfere.

Moving quietly, he rose and carried her water bottle and half-eaten sandwich over to the area she had claimed for her workspace in the basement. He set them nearby but out of the way before returning to finish his own lunch.

When he needed to get back to work, Hawking stopped to drop a kiss on the top of Celeste's head before walking to the elevator. She didn't stop what she was working on but reached over to pick up her water bottle and take a drink.

He smiled all the way to the security office.

Chapter Fourteen

"Cuddle Bug, it's time to call it a night."

Celeste looked up at Hawking and tried to pull her thoughts together. "I just need a few more hours."

"You'll have hours tomorrow. Make a note for yourself where you need to start tomorrow."

Reading the determination in his expression, Celeste pulled up a note and typed furiously before closing her computer with a definite snap of anger. She stood and immediately ran for the bathroom as her stretch made her realize how badly she needed to pee. Working always did that to her. She lost track of all the normal things she needed to do.

When she walked back, Hawking leaned against the table where she'd worked all afternoon. "Will it be looking at pretties or a run?"

"Umm. I'm so stiff I think a run would be better for me," she suggested.

"Let's go get changed," Hawking invited.

"You're going with me?" she said, completely taken by

surprise. Hawking was totally fit, but he was built like a rugby or America football player.

"She doesn't think you can keep up with her," Rocco pointed out.

"Don't you have anyone to parade across the climbing path on the bluff?" Hawking asked.

"That would be fun to try," Celeste murmured.

"I'll be glad to take you out sometime, Little girl," Rocco promised her.

"Maybe you could tempt Sadie to give it a second try," Magnus called, getting up from his chair to walk to the exercise area.

Celeste watched him stretch. He was tired of sitting, too. Instantly, she really wanted to get some fresh air. "Can we go now?" she asked.

"Definitely."

When they got upstairs, Celeste sighed as she looked at the contents of her dresser. In the rush to grab clothes at her apartment, she had only packed a few exercise outfits. Both were dirty. Shrugging, she picked a pair of sleep shorts she had and her most supportive bra.

"Try these, Little girl."

She seized the pile of clothing he plopped down in front of her. Diving in, she found several pairs of colorful, lightweight running shorts and tops. With a cry of happiness, she held three sports bras overhead and danced in a circle as he chuckled.

"Now, I know the way to your heart—pretty running gear. Choose your favorites, and let's put them on."

In a few minutes, she stood dressed in front of him. "How do I look?"

"Like a lean, mean, running machine. Let me put some shorts on. How about new running shoes?" he asked.

"What?" She was filled with excitement.

"Go check that pile," he said, pointing her toward boxes that awaited her attention.

"How did you get all the right sizes?" she asked.

"I unpacked for you, remember? There should be socks there, too."

Amazed that he had thought of all the things she'd need, tears welled into her eyes. Lowering herself onto the floor, Celeste tried to let the tears run down her cheeks silently as she pulled on socks and shoes. A sob escaped from her mouth, and in a flash, he was seated next to her.

"Cuddle Bug? Why are you crying?"

She crawled onto his lap, wrapped her arms and legs around him, and held on tightly. "How did I get so lucky to find you? My whole life crumbled around me, and you were there to pick up the pieces."

"Want to know the truth?" he asked, tilting her back a bit so he could look into her face. Hawking gently wiped away her tears. "I would do anything to keep you from being caught in the middle of this mess—anything but keep your brilliant mind from helping so many. Your company's actions were criminal. I have to admit a fraction of me is glad they acted like they did so I can hold you in my arms. I shouldn't think about myself now, but I'm selfish when it comes to being with you."

All sorts of emotions sped through her brain as she absorbed his words. Finally, she decided what her best answer would be. Leaning forward, she pressed her lips to his in a kiss that quickly escalated. The heat between them flared hot as he tasted her. When she leaned back, they were both breathing faster.

"Thank you, Daddy," she whispered.

"You're welcome, Little girl."

He moved her slightly to the side and put her left shoe, still resting in the box, onto her foot. After tying the laces snugly, he asked, "Ready to go run?"

"Yes, Sir."

"Daddy will do," he said with a wink before getting up and tugging her to stand next to him.

"Yes, Daddy."

"Good girl. You'll have to walk in front of me until I get myself back in control," he mentioned casually.

"Why?" She ran her gaze over his body and stopped at waist level. "Oh!"

"Don't stare at it. You'll never get to run."

"Oh!" Celeste looked at the ceiling and fought herself from checking out the front of his pants. *Damn*!

"You're thinking about it. That doesn't help," he said, his tone wry.

"Of course, I'm thinking about it. It's like the elephant in the room."

Laughing, he went into the bathroom and returned, holding a small towel in front of him. She fought her desire to look down, knowing exactly what preceded him as he walked out. Her panties were already soaked.

"Let's go, CB," he said, putting a hand on her back to guide her to the door, holding the towel in front of him as a shield in the guise of simply an exercise necessity. Some people did carry something to wipe away the sweat as they ran.

In front of him now, she didn't have to struggle to keep her eyes focused on anything else other than the huge bulge tenting his shorts. As they stepped into the elevator, the mirrors caught her gaze. "Holy hell!" she cursed, looking up at the ceiling and finding a mirror there, too.

His laugh went straight to her core. The sound was

deep and masculine; she loved his amusement. As big and stern as he looked to someone who didn't know him, Hawking had a tender and humorous side when you got to know him.

They walked out of the main building and away from people before Hawking nodded to her. "Go, Little girl."

Testing out his speed, she jogged for a few yards. When he seemed at ease, she increased her pace to a slow run. Hawking remained easily at her side. She debated speeding up even more to test him but pushed that out of her mind.

Allowing herself to relax into the motion, Celeste didn't worry about her surroundings. She was with Hawking. He'd take care of any problems. When they approached the back gate, she asked, "Can we go a bit farther?"

"Not ready to go back?" he asked.

"No. Just a half mile or so? Can we go out the gate? Who knows if everyone in the resort area is safe anyway? The bad guys could be in here, too."

"Let's go to that stop sign and come back," he suggested, pointing about a half mile ahead of them.

Instantly, the feeling of being trapped diminished. The resort was gorgeous, but she didn't like feeling restricted. She smiled as they ran the short distance to the sign.

"Celeste! Turn around and run for the gate as fast as you can," Hawking yelled.

Confused by his sudden command, she stopped to look around and froze in place. A group of men appeared from the trees on her left. They rapidly converged on her location. A slap on her butt shocked her from the feeling of being glued in place.

As she spun around, Hawking moved between her and the men streaming toward them. Just up ahead, the Danger Bluff gates promised some form of security. Her heart beat wildly in her chest. She was almost back inside the resort grounds.

A jerk almost knocked Celeste off her feet. "No! Let me go!" One of the men had a handful of her shirt and tried to haul her backward. Her shoes skidded on pieces of gravel scattered on the pavement. She couldn't get any traction. He was too strong.

"Fight, Celeste! I'm coming."

Hawking's voice made her strike out. Pounding on the arm that held her and towed her away, Celeste tried to break his hold. To her surprise, it worked. Suddenly free, she danced backward, moving out of his range before turning to run. She dodged his lunge to recapture her and felt his fingertips brush over her upper arm.

The man fell back, and Celeste saw Hawking take another swing.

"Go, CB. Go!" Hawking yelled.

Celeste ran as fast as she could. She could hear the grunts and thuds of the fight behind her. Even though frightened for Hawking and wanting to help, she followed his instructions. She burst through the opening onto Danger Bluff land and took off for the main building, waving her arms to attract Magnus's attention. She knew he would be monitoring the grounds.

Thank goodness, most of the guests were at dinner. She tried to erase the terror from her face so she didn't alarm them. Who could she get to help Hawking?

Phoenix appeared and raced past her. "Keep going. Get in the basement."

She skidded to a stop at the resort's entrance, not wishing to make a scene. Something inside her told her the fewer people who noticed her, the better. Spotting Sadie behind the desk, Celeste looked at her, letting her see the panic in her gaze. Sadie immediately called someone to take her place. Moving to Celeste's side, Sadie wrapped an arm around her to guide Celeste to the service elevator and jumped inside with her.

"Are you okay?" Sadie asked urgently, running her hands up and down Celeste's arms as she checked to ensure her friend was okay. "Oh. Your shirt is torn!"

"They jumped us. A bunch of guys. Hawking sent me back. He's still there."

"Is he alone?" Sadie asked urgently.

"Phoenix ran past me to help. There were a bunch of guys, like four. They're outnumbered," Celeste shared, wringing her hands.

"Four to Hawking wouldn't have been outnumbered. Four to Hawking and Phoenix? That's a walk in the park," Sadie reassured her as the doors opened into the basement.

"Are you okay, Celeste?" Magnus stood at the entrance.

"I'm okay, but Hawking's still out there."

"Those would-be goons took off when they spotted Phoenix running to join the party. They're on the way back. Come sit down."

The girls settled on the couch. Sadie sat close with her arm around Celeste as she shivered in reaction to the encounter.

Celeste's brain whirled inside her head. Those guys had been after her. If Hawking hadn't been there...

"Why are they doing this?" Celeste asked, not really talking to anyone and feeling absolutely bewildered.

"The knowledge in your head must be astronomically valuable," Sadie guessed.

"I've got to figure out a way to announce my findings to the world in a way that they can't prevent," Celeste muttered. All thoughts faded from her mind as the elevator dinged and the doors opened to reveal Hawking and Phoenix.

Without thinking, Celeste jumped to her feet and ran to leap into Hawking's arms. "Daddy!"

He caught her securely and hugged her slender body to his. "It's okay, Cuddle Bug. I'm here."

"I didn't want to leave you."

"You did exactly what I told you to do. You're safe. I'm fine, and Phoenix got to scare the bad guys. They saw him running and took off. I tried to snag one to question, but he got away."

"He tore my shirt!" Celeste reported.

"I'll get you another shirt," Hawking promised, rubbing a comforting hand up and down her back. "You're safe now. I should have never allowed us to run past the gates. They were waiting for us."

He carried her over to sit on the couch with her cuddled on his lap. She wiggled to get comfortable on his hard thighs as she searched him for injuries. Finding him unharmed, she relaxed against his chest.

"How is this ever going to end?" she muttered.

"We'll figure out a way. In the meantime, you're going to stay safe here with me," Hawking stated.

"I can't even go running," she moaned. "I'll go stir crazy locked in this basement. Can't we just call the police?"

"That will just put you in the spotlight, Little girl," Caesar said, shaking his head.

Celeste sighed. The first time she'd called, the police hadn't helped her much. They were right.

"You'll have to use my secret weapon," Magnus suggested. He pointed toward an industrial treadmill by the exercise equipment. A large screen hung on the wall above it. "I have a trail set in the hills in Hawaii that is synced to the incline of the machine. It's as close as you'll get to running outside."

"Really? That's...neat. I'd try that even if I could go outside," she said, smiling for the first time since she'd returned to the basement. "Thanks, Magnus."

"I'll coordinate a few more paths for us. You might get tired of being on another island," Magnus suggested.

"Thanks, Magnus," Hawking said, grateful for the computer guy's skills.

"No problem. If there's a Little out there twisted enough to want me for her Daddy, it appears I'll need everyone's help as well," Magnus suggested.

"Oh, there's someone out there for you, Magnus," Celeste stated firmly. "I doubt she's even twisted."

As if unable to help himself, Magnus asked, "Why?"

Celeste looked at Sadie, who nodded. "We won't tell anyone, but you're the nicest guy here. Kinda like the team babysitter—or mom. You're always watching out for everyone."

"Magnus is mom!" Phoenix about fell out of his chair laughing while Magnus simply shook his head and muttered, "Littles. They like everyone."

Their giggles dispersed the lingering haze of danger in everyone's expression.

Chapter Fifteen

Pizza from the stone ovens at the resort filled their stomachs for dinner that night as they watched a movie. The two Littles had stared at the pile of pizza boxes that had arrived and swore there was no way just the eight of them could eat that many slices. Hawking deliberately chose a light-hearted comedy that made everyone laugh as they inhaled the cheesy treats.

"Can you really eat another piece?" Celeste whispered when Hawking leaned back against the couch with another in his hand.

"Oh, yeah. Easily. I might need more. Ouch!"

"I just wanted to check to see if there was any more room in there for pizza," Celeste explained, poking his hard abdomen again.

"Be nice to your Daddy. He had a hard day today," Hawking reminded her.

"*You* had a hard day? Some guy grabbed me and tore my new shirt. Then, you smacked me on the butt and yelled at me to run."

"You didn't move when I told you the first time," he reminded her.

"I was scared," she whispered. Big tears gathered in her eyes and rolled down her face.

"Oh, CB. It had to be frightening," Hawking soothed as he dropped the pizza on the box and gathered his Little girl into his arms.

"I was afraid just seeing Celeste's face," Sadie whispered.

Hawking looked over to see her crying as well. Rocco shot him a dirty look and lifted his Little onto his lap. Hawking sent him an apologetic look as he rocked Celeste.

"I think it's past my Little girl's bedtime. If you'll excuse me." Hawking stood to carry Celeste to the elevator.

"I want to go to bed, too, Daddy," Sadie requested, and Rocco immediately stood to follow Hawking with her cradled in his arms.

The ride to the top floor was quiet as the two men walked toward their rooms. Celeste pushed at Hawking's chest. "Put me down, Daddy."

Lowering Celeste to her feet, he watched Rocco do the same. The two Littles raced toward each other and exchanged hugs before returning to their Daddies' sides.

"Night, Sadie."

"Night, Celeste. Sleep well."

Hawking took his Little girl's hand and walked her back to the door. A carefully colored black cat picture was taped on the wood. Celeste walked forward to look at it and touched the paper carefully.

"This wasn't here earlier. Who did this?" she asked.

"It's magic. It must have appeared while we were gone. Maybe our door was jealous of Sadie's penguin."

"I bet. If I were a door, I'd want a picture, too."

"Come on, Celeste. Let's take a shower and go to bed."

"Are you going to sleep now, too?" she asked.

"I'm wiped out as well," he said as he ushered her through the door.

"Were you scared, Daddy?"

"I was very worried that I would lose you," he admitted, pulling her close to wrap his arms around her in a giant bear hug.

"Is this ever going to go away?"

"Yes. We're going to figure out how to handle this best. I promise. For now, we're going to get ready for bed and let our brains rest."

"And my heart. I swear it went a hundred miles an hour when that guy grabbed me."

"Maybe a thousand for me, CB," Hawking exaggerated.

Taking her hand, Hawking led her into the bathroom. "This shirt goes in the trash," he announced, pulling her torn shirt off and tossing it into the garbage.

She shuddered and admitted, "I don't ever want to see that again."

Without rushing, Hawking took her remaining garments off. He led her to the shower and turned it on. "Give it a minute to warm up. I'm going to take this trash away."

Scooping up the container, he walked to the main kitchen to dump it down the trash shoot. As he returned, he heard a giggle from inside Rocco's apartment. Hawking smiled and made a mental note to get a thicker door or avoid playing next to the barrier.

He would never have thought he'd find his Little, much less that he would team up with a group he already felt linked to and find out they were wired the same way he was. Just how much did Baldwin Kingsley know about them? Hawking shook his head in disbelief. Maybe he didn't want to know.

The splash of water captured his attention as he walked

back into the bathroom. He caught glimpses of her attractive shape as he looked through the foggy glass to see Celeste rotating under the warm spray. He quickly took off his clothes and shoes. One thudded to the floor.

Her hand wiped through the fog on the glass as Celeste asked, "Daddy?"

"It's me, Cuddle Bug. You're okay."

She didn't answer but continued to watch him through the glass until it steamed back up. Stalking forward, he stepped into the shower and eased around her.

"You're hogging the water," she complained.

"Let me lather you up, Little girl, and then you can rinse off." He squirted liquid into his palm and spread it over her body. Trying to remain unaffected by the sight and feel of her wet body was impossible, but he tried to ignore his desires.

"Daddy?" When he didn't respond quickly enough, she repeated, "Daddy? Can I touch it?"

Hawking couldn't ignore her the second time. "Daddy's cock isn't a toy, Little girl."

"I'll be really careful. Playing with it will make me forget about the mean men who tried to abduct me," Celeste urged.

Whisking his fingers over her taut nipples, Hawking reminded her. "Daddy's already distracting you."

"Scientific studies have proven that women multitask better than males. They even suggest women need more things happening at once."

"You better not be involved in any of that kind of scientific research, Little girl."

"What kind?" she asked, perplexed.

"The playing with penises kind."

She grinned at him. "It would all be in the pursuit of knowledge."

"Knowledge, huh?" He tried to keep his lips from curving

and failed miserably. "Here." He squirted liquid soap into her hand. "You wash Daddy, and I'll get you clean."

Hawking knew this was a terrible idea when she immediately wrapped her slick hands around his shaft, studiously spreading lather over his cock. He bit his tongue to keep from groaning when she pulled from root to tip. Her experiment in the reverse made his hips buck forward automatically.

"Whoa, Daddy," she soothed.

"Daddy is not a horse. Don't say it," he warned, lifting one finger when she opened her mouth. He knew exactly what comparison she planned to make next between his penis and an equine one.

"All I need to say is neigh!" she said, bursting into laughter.

When her hands automatically squeezed his thickness, Hawking moaned before tugging her fingers from holding him and whirling her around to press her breasts and tummy against the cool tiles.

"It's cold, Daddy," she complained, wiggling delectably in front of him.

With absolutely no mercy, Hawking spread the liquid soap all over her back. Cupping her bottom, he molded his palms to her toned buttocks and glided his fingers across the sensitive skin. He hesitated at the small entrance and swirled his fingers around the tight ring of muscles.

"No, Daddy."

"Maybe I should make some scientific studies of my own," he teased, pushing his fingertip inside.

"It stings! The soap burns inside."

"I should use something different as a lubricant to slide into you," he suggested.

"Yes!"

Hawking smiled. He would be glad to remind her of this

eager agreement. "Okay, CB." He slid his finger from her and rinsed his hand in the spray before grabbing the handheld showerhead and thoroughly rinsing off the suds.

"Daddy," she moaned, lifting her bottom up for his attention.

"Spread your legs, CB."

He waited for her to process his request. Slowly she stepped her legs apart. "More, Little girl."

As she moved, he glided a hand between her body and the tiled wall that had warmed from her body heat. Stroking over her skin, he moved his fingers into the slick juices that had gathered between her legs. She might deny the bottom play was arousing, but his Little girl loved to be dominated there. He explored her pink folds, caressing her as he pointed the spray attachment upward between her legs.

"Ooo!" she moaned as she froze in place. Her fingers curled against the hard surface below them as she struggled to stay in place.

"Good girl. You are so beautifully made, Cuddle Bug. Should I let you come now?" he asked, flicking the shower-head away from her pussy.

"Yes. Put it back. Please!"

That last word became three syllables as he focused the spray back on her. Hawking brushed his fingers over her clit as he bit the sensitive spot on her neck where it met her shoulder.

"Ahhh!" Her head reared back as her body became completely rigid.

Gentling his touch and directing the spray away, Hawking gathered her body against him. He used the hand sprayer to make sure she was free of suds and then hung it up, directing the water flow toward the tiles. Moving her out of the shower spray, Hawking wrapped her in a towel and helped her step out of the enclosure.

"Go sit on the tub, CB. I'll be right there to dry you off."

To his delight, she walked directly to the tub and sat on the side, watching him. Restoring the direction of the water, he quickly washed his body and wrapped a towel around his waist before turning off the shower.

As he walked forward, Celeste stood and dropped her towel. She tugged his off and tossed it to the side. Without saying a word, she took his hand and walked him to the bed. Crawling onto the bedspread, she reached for the nightstand drawer and opened it to retrieve a small packet.

Holding it out to him, she asked, "Please, Daddy. I need you inside me."

He'd never be able to resist that invitation. Hawking quickly donned the condom on his erection and crawled over her, pressing kisses and caressing her damp skin. Her eyes were half shuttered with passion but fixed on him as he fitted the head of his cock to her opening.

"Fast or slow, Little girl?"

"Slow."

He felt the edges of his mouth curl upward. He'd exhaust her with pleasure before she collapsed into sleep. Pushing forward, he filled her and paused, letting her adjust to his size. Her tight heat tantalized him.

When her fingers held on to his shoulders as he moved, he seduced and pleasured her with long, slow strokes aimed to glide just where she needed it. Celeste wrapped her legs around his hips, fully opening herself to his thrusts, and he reached deeper inside her body.

Chapter Sixteen

Waking up the next morning sprawled over Hawking's hard body, Celeste smiled and pressed a kiss to his hard chest. She might have to rethink her aversion to going to bed early. Their lovemaking had continued for a very long time the previous night.

"Good morning, Little girl," Hawking said in a deep, sleepy voice that made her happy.

"Good morning, Daddy."

"Did you have any bad dreams?"

"No. You made me focus on other things," she said, feeling her cheeks heat slightly.

"I'm glad. I didn't have any nightmares either," he said, grinning at her.

Catching sight of the time, he cursed, "Damn it. I have to get up, CB."

Hawking eased her off his body and asked, "Do you want to get up now or be a slug in bed?"

"Bed," she said, yawning and settling on her tummy. His

hand smoothed over her hair before she felt him kiss her temple.

"Sleep, Cuddle Bug. No going out into the resort. Stay here or go work on your research in the basement with Magnus."

A horrifying thought leaped into her mind. She pushed her torso up to turn around to look at him. "Magnus can't see us in here, can he?"

"Not in my apartment. He doesn't have eyes on any of the private areas. The changing rooms, bathrooms, and bedrooms are all off-limits."

"Thank goodness," she muttered, collapsing back to the mattress.

His eyes narrowed. "No touching yourself while I'm gone, Little girl. Your orgasms belong to me now."

"Always?" she asked, pushing herself up once again to watch him as he pulled on his clothes.

"Always. Daddy will monitor you when you masturbate from now on," he said firmly.

"You want to watch me?"

"Oh, yeah. If you're good, I'll let you watch me," he teased.

An instant image popped into her mind as she stared at him, which left her unable to think of a reply.

"Be good." Hawking stopped to kiss her deeply.

Between the kiss and the mental picture in her head of Hawking touching himself, there was no way she could fall back to sleep. Her hands crept down her abdomen and froze inches from their target.

Your orgasms belong to me now.

Groaning, she rolled over on her stomach and buried her head in the soft pillow. Having a Daddy was going to kill her.

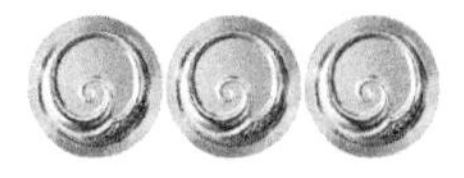

An hour later, she forced herself out of bed and took a cold shower. With her desire somewhat banked by the frigid water, she dressed quickly and brushed her hair and teeth. She wanted to talk to Hawking but knew he'd be in the security office, and that was a no-no.

Taking the elevator downstairs, she allowed Magnus to bully her into eating a few bites of breakfast, and then Celeste dived into work. Her goal was to organize her research data so it would be easily replicated and understood. She carefully supported any hypotheses she'd had in moving from one stage to another in the process. Celeste felt like she was buried to her eyebrows in work when Magnus interrupted her for lunch.

"Take a break. Come eat a sandwich," he invited from across the room.

"Sorry. I can't right now."

In what seemed like five minutes later, her Daddy stood beside her. "You have thirty seconds to wrap up that sentence."

"I can't stop now. Give me an hour," she requested without looking up. Celeste tried not to be annoyed by his disruption.

"You now have fifteen seconds."

Something in his tone made Celeste make a checkmark in the margin where she was working. She jotted three words—check repeat sequence. That would give her a clue for what she had been doing.

Looking up this time, she asked, "What? I'm busy. You can't just interrupt me in the middle of work, Hawking."

"That's two infractions, Little girl. Tone and name. Don't get three."

Exasperated, she dared ask, "What are you going to do? Spank me in front of everyone?"

"Three and no." Hawking pulled her chair back.

Celeste grabbed for the edge of the table and barely missed. By the look on his face, she knew that was lucky. In one easy haul that made the world seem to spin around her, Hawking lifted Celeste from the chair and draped her over his shoulder. She bounced on his shoulder as he walked across the room.

He made one stop along the way before continuing on his path. She wondered what had stopped him but saw a tray of sandwiches on the table when he passed. He was hungry?

"Don't let *me* interrupt your lunch," she said sarcastically.

"I ate lunch approximately three hours ago." He informed her before announcing, "Four."

"Doesn't the countdown stop at three?" she said in the same disrespectful tone.

"Five."

A bit of self-preservation kicked in, and Celeste bit her lower lip to keep herself from spouting off anything else as the elevator doors opened and Hawking stepped inside.

The car seemed to crawl slowly upward, stretching out the tension. Celeste wanted to cover her ears to block out the elevator music that seemed loud in the silence that filled the small space. She tried to peek into the mirrors that lined the inside to see Hawking's face, but the angle of their bodies prevented that. Bouncing against his hard shoulder as he walked, Celeste stared at the carpet under his feet. Remorse flooded into her.

As he opened the door to his apartment, she stuttered, "I'm sorry!"

"It's a bit late for that, Miss I'm-going-to push-Daddy-all-the-way-to-five."

She swallowed hard at the sound of his voice. Hard and determined, Celeste knew she'd truly messed up. When he stood her in front of him and took a seat on the bed, she fled for the door.

"If you run away from me now, I will keep you safe but will understand you don't think I'm your Daddy."

"What? Just because I didn't eat one of those?" she gestured to the wrapped item lying on the bed a short distance from him. He'd picked up a sandwich from the stack?

"Because you can't allow yourself to let someone take care of you."

"Maybe I'm not hungry," she rebelled.

Growl!

Celeste looked down at her abdomen and poked it for betraying her. When she looked up, she found him simply watching her. "Okay! So, I've been hungry. I couldn't take a break. I needed to keep working."

"The best thing about sandwiches is they were created to eat while doing something else," he said, his tone deadly even.

"I don't need to hear the old fable about the Earl of Sandwich," she said in exasperation.

"Nor do you need a nutritional lecture on brain chemistry and the need for food."

She stared at him, trying to come up with an answer to that. There wasn't one. "Okay. You're right. I should've eaten a sandwich."

"I'm also right about you being my Little girl. Would you agree with that, too?"

The last of her anger fizzled away. "Yes," she whispered.

"And that makes you my Little to take care of."

She nodded, looking down at the carpet.

"Come stretch over my lap, Celeste. Then you'll eat the sandwich and take a nap."

"But..."

"No buts except for the one you're going to show your Daddy."

Celeste dragged her toes as she walked forward to stand next to him. She wanted to run away as he unfastened her jeans, but she steeled her spine to stay in place. Shivering as he tugged her jeans and panties down to her ankles, she waited for his next directions.

He silently helped her over his lap, his silence making the tension rise inside her. *How mad is he?*

Hawking tapped lightly on her skin, spreading his touch all over. The staccato slaps kept her jumping as she never knew what to expect. When would he spank her for real?

"What did you do incorrectly, Little girl?"

"I didn't eat when you told me to. Then, I acted badly."

"You acted like a young woman who hadn't had anything to eat for a long time. You were tired and cranky," he clarified.

With that statement complete, he swatted her fully, drawing a gasp from her lips. He scattered her punishment across her bottom as she tried to twist and turn in all directions to avoid the next one. Hawking easily held her in place. The material bunched around her ankles hampered her movements.

Realizing she could have avoided everything if she hadn't been so stubborn, Celeste melted over his lap, accepting her punishment as tears started to roll down her cheeks. "I'm sorry, Daddy."

"Count down the last ten with me, Cuddle Bug."

"What?"

"Count with me, and your spanking will be over. Ten."

When she didn't count, he swatted her again and repeated himself. "Ten."

"Ten!" she said quickly.

"Good girl. Nine."

"Ouch, Daddy! Nine!"

They counted the last few together, and Hawking rubbed her red skin, soothing her as she dangled from his hard thighs. "That's my sweet Little girl. Will you come snuggle with Daddy?" he invited.

"Please," she whispered and gasped when the world whirled around as he lifted her to sit on her punished bottom. "I'm sorry I was bad, Daddy."

"Will you stop and listen to me next time?" he asked.

"Yes!" she said with such conviction that she surprised herself.

"I'm glad, Little girl."

Hawking wiped the tears from her face with his shirt and hugged her close to his body. When her breath steadied, he reached down to remove her shoes and the wadded material from her ankles. Reaching to his side, he picked up the sandwich and opened the plastic baggie it was wrapped inside to hand to her.

Resting her head on his broad shoulder, Celeste devoured the sandwich and felt the empty feeling inside her ease. He'd made everything better.

Well, except for my bottom.

Chapter Seventeen

Waking up with Hades snuggling under her chin, Celeste blinked her eyes. She rose on one forearm to look at the black cat clock hanging on the wall in her playroom. Two hours had passed in a flash. She laid her head back on the pillow and smiled.

After her spanking, Hawking had carried her into the small attached room. She'd almost cried again at seeing the beautiful comforter stretched over the bed. He'd obviously taken a break from his duties to make her bed and unpack a few of her boxes.

After pulling back the soft cover, her Daddy had tucked her in bed with Hades and had stayed by her side, brushing his fingers through her hair until she'd allowed herself to fall asleep. She reached a hand to touch her bottom. It was still warm to the touch and ouchy. She would be standing to type up her documentation tonight.

"You're awake. You had a good nap. I bet you feel better," Hawking's deep voice sounded from the doorway.

"I do. I didn't know I was tired," she admitted.

"Your brain is working overtime, CB."

"I know." She looked down at the comforter and plucked at the surface. "I'm sorry, Daddy."

"I know you are. You don't need to dwell on mistakes. Spankings erase all the bad feelings. They give you a new beginning."

"You're not mad at me?" she asked, peeking up at him.

"Not at all. Unless you plan on skipping a lunch break tomorrow...?"

"No! I'll stop and take a break. I promise."

"That's my Little girl."

"Can I talk to the team?" she asked.

"Of course. Everyone's gathering for dinner. It's fish and chips night."

"That means French fries, right? Can I just call them that? I mean, do I say chips even when I'm dining with people from the United States?"

"Yes. We're learning to be New Zealanders. Want to go down to hang with everyone?"

"Are they going to laugh at me? I bet they know you spanked me."

"They probably know I spanked you, but I'm equally certain no one will laugh at you. Did you deserve it?" he asked.

She took a deep breath and let it out before forcing herself to answer. "Yes. I wouldn't listen."

"They're all Daddies, and Sadie, being a Little, understands spankings."

"Do you think Rocco spanks her?" Celeste asked, pushing herself to sit on her bottom.

"That's between Sadie and her Daddy."

"That's a yes," Celeste muttered.

"Come on, Cuddle Bug. Let's go down and enjoy a break from working. All work and no play makes Celeste..." Hawking deliberately let his voice drift away as he looked at her.

"Makes Celeste's bottom ouchy."

"Exactly." Hawking walked to the closet and pulled out a full skirt with an elastic waist. It was shades of the rainbow and very pretty.

Celeste threw back the covers eagerly and froze, remembering she only had socks on the lower part of her body. She moved Hades to cover her nakedness.

"Daddy has seen and tasted pretty much every inch of your body. The bits I've missed, I have a date with to remedy that lack," Hawking reminded her.

Feeling silly, she laid Hades on the pillow and scooted to the edge of the bed, where she wiggled her sore bottom. Celeste stood and felt very Little. Half dressed in front of her Daddy, who still wore his work attire, the difference underlined the power exchange she craved. He was in control. She was not.

"Raise your hands, Little girl," he directed, threading the skirt over her head and down to her waist.

She looked over her body and smiled. It was so pretty and soft. It didn't hurt her bottom at all. That thought made her look up at him. "I need panties, Daddy."

"Nope. Spanked bottoms need extra air to heal."

"I'm going to go down to dinner naked?" she squeaked.

"You're wearing a T-shirt, bra, skirt, and socks. That doesn't qualify as naked," he reminded her.

"But underneath..." she whispered.

"It will be our secret."

She walked over to look in the mirror, turning this way and that way. The skirt was full, and all the layers were thick enough that no one would be able to tell.

"Can we come back and open all the presents?" she asked, afraid he'd send everything back.

"I think that would be a great idea. There are so many things left to discover." He held out his hand and led her to the elevator.

Trying to distract herself from the chilly air fluttering around her bare skin under the floaty skirt, she said, "I liked my water bottle today."

"Good. Let's pick it up while we're in the basement and clean it so it will be ready for tomorrow. What fruit do you want to try next?"

"Strawberries and lemons."

"Hmm, like strawberry lemonade," he guessed.

"Yes. I think that will be yummy."

"I'll have to try a sip," Hawking murmured.

"You can drink from my bottle, too, Daddy. I'll share."

"Thank you, Cuddle Bug."

The doors opened to reveal everyone was there. Sadie carefully held plates and walked around the large table designed to accommodate a crowd to set a plate in front of each chair. "Hi, Celeste. The food's supposed to be ready in just a few minutes. The kitchen just sent the five-minute warning."

"I'll run up and get the cart," Phoenix offered. He pushed the button and disappeared into the elevator.

Celeste walked slowly to the table, trying not to ruffle her skirt too much. "Can I help?" she asked Sadie.

"Would you like to put a napkin next to each plate?"

The Little girls made circles around the table to add

knives, forks, and spoons. They were giggling by the time the last piece of silverware was in place. It was a fun game.

"Thank you, Littles. Phoenix will be back in a minute. Are you hungry?" Caesar asked after coming to admire the table.

Yeses burst from their lips, and they giggled at each other.

Almost everyone settled at the table and chatted. Magnus finally joined them, saying, "He's in the elevator."

When the doors opened, the delicious scent of freshly fried fish and chips filled the air. "I almost just stopped the elevator between the floors and had a feast," Phoenix confessed.

"I have control of the elevator," Magnus said, narrowing his eyes.

"Good thing I didn't try that then," Phoenix said, then laughed.

"Do you ever get tired of watching the world happen around you?" Celeste asked. When Magnus looked at her with a funny expression on his face, she added, "I'm in my lab all the time. Sometimes, it seems like I come out and the seasons have changed, or I've missed a holiday, and all the Christmas candy is on sale. You know—like life is passing me by."

"That's sad. You need to get away from your research more," Sadie said before turning to Hawking with a meaningful look.

He nodded, acknowledging her message.

"Don't get me wrong," Celeste said quickly. "I would have never made all the progress I have if I wasn't completely dedicated to my efforts. My brain always reminds me there are real-world problems that are more important than frivolous activities like binge-watching movies." Celeste seized on their activity the previous evening when she struggled to think of something to use as an example.

"I like movies," Sadie said, twirling a fry in the air and then giggling when Rocco captured her hand and took a bite. "Hey!"

"I enjoyed the movie last night. I can't tell you the last one I saw," Celeste confessed.

"It is possible to balance work and play in your life," Hawking suggested.

"Maybe...?" she said, shrugging.

"You can choose the movie tonight if you'd like," Caesar suggested.

"Oh, Daddy and I have a bunch of packages to unpack in my... In his room," Celeste covered for herself, hoping her cheeks didn't look as red as they felt.

"Celeste, all the rooms on the top floor are identical," Rocco shared.

"Really?" she squeaked.

"I'll show you my playroom if you'll show me yours," Sadie said. "I saw the black cat Hawking colored in the security office to put on your door. He did a really good job."

"You did that yourself? I thought you found it somewhere." Celeste turned to look at her Daddy in astonishment.

"Colored pencils are too appealing to ignore. Maybe we can have an art night?" Hawking suggested.

"I like to paint rocks," Kestrel said.

"Really? What do you do with them?"

His lips curved at the corners. "I set them around in places for people to find. It's a day brightener for most people."

"That sounds like fun. Could you teach us?" Celeste asked.

"Of course. I'd love to have more hands creating fun,"

Kestrel offered. "I was up in the helicopter yesterday, and I saw what looked like a family gathered around the edge of the fountain. I knew immediately someone had found the parrot rock I set down there."

"Do you try to hide them?" Sadie asked.

"No. I just put them in plain sight. It's amazing how many people walk right over something without seeing it, but kids find them instantly."

"I'm going to start looking," Phoenix said.

Celeste felt her heart sink. She was stuck inside. She'd never get the chance to look for a painted rock.

Her Daddy wrapped his arm around her. "This won't last forever, Cuddle Bug. You'll get to go outside again."

"Promise?"

"Promise. Now, have you finished eating?"

"Yes. Can we go open boxes?" she asked eagerly, shaking off her sadness.

"If you all will excuse us, we'll head upstairs to see if Celeste likes everything I ordered."

They stood and walked hand in hand to the elevator. Just as the doors opened, Celeste remembered and tugged her hand away to run to her research area and grab her water bottle. A formula caught her eye, and she almost got sucked back into working.

"Little girl," her Daddy called from the elevator.

"Coming."

On their way up, she looked at the numbers breezing past on the screen. "How come no one ever gets on the elevator with us?"

"Magnus has it set so it doesn't pick up passengers if the fifth floor or basement is selected. He can have it stop for guests if they happen to be in the elevator when one of us gets in, but it will never go to the basement or fifth floor with anyone other than us."

Once in her playroom, Celeste oohed and aahed over all the amazing things Hawking had ordered for her. She was very relieved he hadn't gotten her another stuffie. Hades didn't play well with others.

Chapter Eighteen

Two days later, Celeste felt ready. She walked to Magnus's desk and asked, "Could you call my Daddy to come down here?"

"Is something wrong?" Magnus looked at her in concern.

"No. It's finally right," she assured him.

A few minutes later, Hawking appeared. "Need to take a break?"

"I've got everything ready to be released, Daddy. I have a plan."

"Tell me."

"Magnus should listen, too. I hope he'll help."

"I'll do what I can, Celeste," Magnus said, adjusting his baseball cap.

"I would like to send a summary of my research to the three largest scientific journals in the world. Whoever jumps first to cover the news can have the research. In addition, I would like to contact all the major television news carriers and provide them with enough information to prove the research exists."

"I'm trying to be supportive, CB, but I have a question. When they release the information, won't your old company simply tell the press that they disproved your research?" Hawking asked.

"That will definitely happen. That's why I'm also going to send the research to several small cancer research teams. They can't have control of every single bit of the scientific world."

Magnus's lips pursed for a moment. "That could work to circumvent their power. Dispersed this widely, it will be difficult to maintain your name on the research. Everyone will want to claim it for themselves. You could lose credit for making this breakthrough, Celeste," he pointed out.

"I need to avoid that and keep my name associated with the research. That's what will keep me safe. If I'm in the spotlight, that will prevent them from targeting me. If I'm reading them right, they won't risk the negative attention that would come with an attack on a highly talked-about scientist."

She paused for a minute before adding, "I did have Magnus file a patent for me through some kind of tech that bounces the signal around to different countries to foil someone if they're watching for me. Who knows? Maybe we can convince them that you snuck me out of the resort without them seeing me."

Clearing her throat, she added, "I have one final step."

"Okay. What's that?" Hawking asked with a smile, letting her know he was impressed with her plans so far.

"I'm counting on the documentation going everywhere to create enough proof that there will be a frenzy for me to appear on the largest morning news shows around the world to share my breakthrough. I plan to share how my research was tampered with and how I was let go from my position."

"Around the world?" Hawking asked. "You're going to

lose a lot of sleep."

"Yes. I'm sorry, Magnus. Can I impose on you as well? I'll need your help to protect the signal from their notice for as long as possible."

"How are you going to convince them you're not just a crazy woman fired from her job?" Magnus asked bluntly.

"I will send them slides displaying my dismissal report and how the research was tampered with to the first news outlets who request interviews. Thankfully, my old employers always do their reports on official paper with their letterhead."

"I'll be here whenever you need me," Magnus said and shook his head in disbelief at her level of preparedness.

"We start tomorrow?" Hawking asked.

Celeste drew a breath and released it, letting her shoulders relax. "I plan to send my research to the scientific community today."

"Let's see what happens. When you have those addresses and the documentation together, send them to me," Magnus said.

"I'll do that now."

Hawking interrupted her path to the computer. "It's going to get bad, Little girl. Don't keep anything from me."

"I promise, Daddy. You'll know everything."

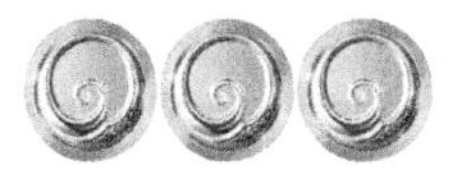

Three hours later, Hawking returned to the basement to check on what was happening. One look at his Little girl, pacing back and forth across the floor, told him she hadn't received any responses.

"Little girl, what would you do if someone claimed to

have the solution to stopping cancer in its tracks?" Hawking asked.

"I'd look at every word, formula, and line."

"How long would that take you?"

"Days," she answered, looking completely depleted.

"It's been three hours. You need something to keep you occupied."

"I'm stuck in here with Magnus."

The computer genius didn't even look up. Hawking figured he hadn't said a single word for several hours. Probably three. "I think you need to get out of this basement. You can come down for a run later if you want, but let's head upstairs, and you can spend some time in your playroom."

As he urged her toward the elevator with a hand at the small of her back, Hawking waited for her next protest.

"There's nothing to do up there."

"I think several things are in the wrong place. Could you look at all the things I unpacked before you helped me and see what you think?"

"You mean, organize it?" she asked as they stepped in through the elevator doors.

"That sounds like work. I think it's more like putting them where you like them best."

"Oh, I could do that. There were a few things in weird places," she confessed.

"It definitely needs your touch."

He dropped her off in the apartment, warning her not to move anything heavy while he wasn't in the room. However, as soon as they reached the door, she was embroiled in scientifically placing the decorations where they would best be seen and enjoyed. Who knew that the vector of vision a person had upon entering would be so important?

Damn, I love her.

Chapter Nineteen

When he went upstairs to check on Celeste, he found her fast asleep on the bed in her playroom. Hawking looked around and smiled. She had completely changed the room around. Following his directions not to move the big furniture, she'd marked the dresser with a pink sock. The matching sock was carefully placed against the far wall.

Leaving quietly, he ran into Kestrel. "Hey! Can you help me move a dresser? We need to be as quiet as possible."

"Lead on. My lips are sealed," Kestrel agreed without asking a single question.

The two men tiptoed into the room, freezing when Celeste mumbled something about cell division and turned over. When she was still, Hawking signaled Kestrel to pick up one side of the dresser and pointed to the pink sock across the room. Within seconds, they had it placed in the spot she had requested.

Kestrel waved and left quietly with a smile. Hawking had a feeling Kestrel would be the next to find his Little. Two out of two were pretty good odds, making everyone suspect that the job they'd be asked to do would lead each of them to their Little.

With one final look at his sleeping Little, Hawking followed Kestrel out. The two men took the elevator down to the main floor together.

"You off on a helicopter tour?" Hawking asked.

"Yes. I wore my glasses back to the hotel yesterday and forgot to take them. It's so sunny out there today, I'd be blind if I tried to pilot the helicopter without them."

"I'm sure the guest will wait for a few minutes if you're late. Thank you for helping me with the dresser. I didn't realize I would delay you further," Hawking apologized.

"No problem. Littles come first."

When the doors opened, Kestrel jogged toward the helicopter pad to join the excursion. Hawking knew he'd show them something special to make up for the short wait. He'd love to have Kestrel take Celeste up to see the resort from the air.

Crossing his fingers, Hawking hoped she would be freed from this threat soon. When his phone signaled thirty seconds later, he expected to hear Celeste's voice. Instead, Magnus's name appeared on his screen.

"What's up, Magnus?"

"I think you and Celeste need to see this. A national news service is broadcasting a cancer cure."

"We'll be there."

Dashing up the stairs when he found the elevator busy, Hawking rushed to the playroom and found Celeste sitting up in bed. *Thank goodness she was awake!*

"Hi, CB. Magnus says something is on TV about a cancer cure."

"Let's watch it!" she cheered, jumping out of bed to rush past Hawking.

He followed her to the common area and flicked on the TV. Luckily, the news was playing on the channel that popped up first.

"...the credit for the discovery is going to Dr. Alan Hughes of the esteemed Rosenburg Research Facility. There are rumors that he is under consideration for the Nobel Prize in Science. This new innovative method of slowing down the division and spread of cancer cells could just be the key to ending cancer, or at least slowing it down significantly while more advances are made."

Celeste looked at him with a bewildered expression in her eyes and blindly sat down on the couch. "I can't believe it."

"Is that your old company?" Hawking asked.

"And my old supervisor. They fired me, told me my research was shit, and stole it."

"What can I do to help?"

"I don't know. I don't know what to do."

"First, they shut you down. You thought it was because they didn't want to lose the prescription income from the cancer patients and the proceeds from insurance payments."

"They probably knew they couldn't shut me up entirely because they couldn't get to me. So, they changed tactics. They've figured out how to profit from this. I need a computer," she said, standing up and walking to the elevator with a single focus.

Hawking joined her and didn't say a word. He could tell by the look on her face that he shouldn't interrupt her. Once they reached the basement, she fled to her computer and powered it on. Needing to do something to support her, he grabbed her water bottle and refilled it with fresh ice water and fruit. He set it quietly by her side and stopped to ask Magnus for a favor.

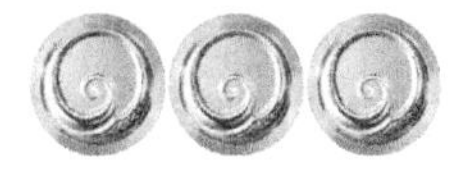

Pouring through the reports, Celeste wanted to bang her head on the table or throw the borrowed computer across the room. Neither one would help her.

An email message popped up on her screen. Exasperated by the annoyance, Celeste scrolled the mouse over it to delete it when she noticed the name. The email account was TakedownDrHughes.

"What?" she asked out loud.

"Everything okay?" Magnus asked.

"I don't know. I just got this message from a weird email account."

"Don't open it. Forward it unopened to me," Magnus demanded and recited his email address.

Seconds later, he read off the screen, "TakedownDrHughes? That sounds ominous. Let me create a secure area to open it safely."

Celeste stood up from her desk and swiftly walked over to look over Magnus's shoulder. His fingers flew over the keyboard, and she watched what he was doing for a short time before totally giving up. She tried to stay calm as she waited for him to finish.

"Do you know someone named Edgar?" Magnus asked.

"Edgar Telafette? He's a leading name in cancer research. He abruptly left the company that fired me. No one knew what happened," Celeste answered, leaning closer over his shoulder to read.

"Sit in my chair, Celeste. I'll bring yours over."

She collapsed into the warm chair as she read.

Dr. Blanke,

I'm sorry to see that Dr. Hughes is up to his old tricks. My discovery that he took credit for was extremely minor compared to your incredible research. I would like you to get the credit for your work.

If you are trying to figure out your next move, I suggest you contact a reporter. Ben Harbin is his name. He has talked with several other scientists who were let go from this firm with allegations of muddy research data or processes immediately before the company announced breakthroughs.

Gather all your evidence on steps where you presented or logged your progress and theories. Applying for a patent was a brilliant step. That takes time and insight to complete fully. There's no way Dr. Hughes got this filed before you did.

Fight this with all you have. Dr. Hughes needs to be stopped.

Edgar Telafette

The scientist had attached a picture of a man and his business card at the bottom of the email. Ben Harbin.

Feeling more hope than she'd felt for days, Celeste turned and looked at Magnus, waiting for him to finish reading the email. "How do I contact this reporter? Can I send a message from my account?"

"You focus on crafting your message to the reporter while I get your Daddy and the rest of the team down here to plot our next move."

"Can you do some kind of background check on this

reporter?" she asked, trying not to leap headfirst into what could be a trap.

"Absolutely next on my list," the computer guru reassured her. He stood and pushed Celeste's chair back to her workstation before returning to the computers.

Celeste tried to think of the best way to provide enough information to the reporter so that he'd know the facts were authentic without giving him too much if he was one of the bad guys.

Hawking appeared before her, and she looked up. "Did Magnus tell you what the company's done?"

"He just told me to get here. Run through whatever it is for me."

Quickly, Celeste brought him up to date. As she finished, she explained, "I'm writing a message to the reporter while Magnus is making sure this isn't a ruse."

"He checks out. He's on staff at the largest English language paper in the world," Magnus reported.

"The largest? That means something, doesn't it?" Celeste asked.

"He could make a big splash with the news. I would suggest you contact him through a secure line. I have one set up for you. Have you figured out what to send?"

"I think I'm going to identify myself as the scientist who completed this research and give him links to the various places where different stages of my work were acknowledged by my former company as well as outside organizations."

"Are you going to mention your patent?" Hawking asked.

"Not now. I don't know how much power they have. Could a patent disappear?" Celeste asked.

"A New Zealand patent? I would think that would be difficult to do," Hawking suggested. He looked over his shoulder at Magnus.

"Anything completed digitally could be erased. But, there would always be footprints left of it," Magnus assured her. "Do you have a confirmation and application number?"

"Yes," Celeste assured him. "I even took a screenshot so I would have it."

"Smart move," Magnus nodded.

"What's up?" Phoenix asked as he, Sadie, and Kestrel stepped out of the elevator.

"Rocco's out at the bluff, climbing, and Caesar's with a group of scuba divers," Sadie reported.

"We'll catch them up soon. Want to tell them the news, Celeste?"

"A colleague of mine sent me the contact information for a reporter investigating a series of scientists who worked at my company and were fired. Dr. Hughes also claimed their discoveries."

"I seriously don't like that guy," Phoenix muttered.

Celeste scowled. "Me, neither."

"Do I invite Ben Harbin here or offer to meet him at a different location if he wants to talk to me personally?" Celeste asked.

"Try to accomplish everything online. If you have to meet, you do so while being interviewed on a national morning news show," Hawking suggested.

"Oh, I don't think it will get that much coverage," Celeste said quickly as her heart rate skyrocketed at the thought of being on TV.

"You discovered a key method to stopping cancer in its tracks. I'd definitely want to hear that," Sadie said confidently.

"I'm going to send the message and see what happens. Keep your fingers crossed for me."

Celeste lifted her hand above her computer and dropped

her finger down on the keyboard to contact the reporter. She could feel everyone's eyes on her as they waited for an answer.

When five long minutes had passed, Celeste shrugged and commented, "Well, that was anticlimactic."

"He could be in the john," Hawking reassured her. "Standing around watching the screen isn't going to speed up his answer. I'm sure he needs to confirm your information."

"We'll get back to work," Sadie suggested, beckoning Phoenix and Kestrel back to the elevator. "Keep us updated."

When it was quiet again in the basement, Hawking asked, "Want to go for a run on the treadmill? I don't think you ever tried Magnus's Hawaiian run."

"Yes. That's exactly what I want to do," Celeste said, seizing on that idea. She definitely didn't wish to hang around waiting for the laptop to notify her that she had a response.

Hawking walked with her to the elevator. Just as the doors closed, a call came in for him from one of the gates. Celeste knew immediately that he would have to go. She smiled at his concerned face.

"Go, Daddy. I know you want to stay with me, but that won't hurry up his answer. You go do security things, and I'll run. I'll let you know as soon as I see a message," she promised.

"I'll come check on you as soon as possible, CB."

"Thanks, Daddy," she said as she exited the elevator on the top floor. Celeste waved goodbye as the doors closed. It surprised her how easy calling him Daddy had become. *That didn't take very long.*

As Celeste changed clothes, she pondered how easily it had been for her to get used to having a Daddy. Hawking made it so easy. He was so nurturing and supportive while tough as nails. This would have been a nightmare without his support—without the whole team, really.

And of all the resorts? How had she been lucky enough to select Danger Bluff? If she hadn't seen that advertisement sent to her email weeks ago, she wouldn't have known it existed. A thought popped into her mind. The guys and Sadie always talked about this Baldwin Kingsley. No one had ever met him, but he seemed to know everything and everyone. He couldn't have known that Dr. Hughes would attack her research with the villainous purpose of stealing it for himself. Maybe he was an investigative reporter. No, that couldn't be right. The team said he had to be super rich to do all the things he did around the world.

She'd gotten a hint that he'd saved all the men from some earlier danger. Making a mental note, she reminded herself to find out what exactly he'd done to help Hawking. He seemed to know a lot about cancer. She hadn't seen any clues that he had ever been sick, but that didn't mean anything. He was so strong and fit. She could see how someone who had battled a disease could become very focused on building muscle and endurance.

After pulling on a tank top over her sports bra, Celeste put on her socks and shoes. Walking out of the apartment into the empty fifth floor, she punched the button on the elevator. A run would do her well. She needed to clear her mind and examine everything from all angles to ensure she wasn't missing anything.

When her thoughts leapfrogged over all the latest events, Celeste considered where she could shift her research focus to next. Eliminating cancer was her life's goal. Her new discovery would require years of testing and retesting before it could be applied to all types of cancer and all patients.

Walking out of the elevator, she waved at Magnus as she

passed him and headed for the large machine. To her delight, he had already set up the program, and all she needed to do was grab her water bottle and step up on the treadmill. With a push of a button, she was off, running through a tropical paradise, giving her brain a much-needed break.

Chapter Twenty

"How long has she been on that thing?" Hawking asked Magnus when he entered the basement after work.

Magnus scowled. "An hour. I've tried to get her attention, but she's zoned out."

She was beet red and dripping with sweat as Hawking reached over and turned the machine off. As it came to a halt, he wrapped an arm around her middle and plucked her off the treadmill.

She squealed, probably from shock. "Hey. I was running."

Hawking kept her back plastered to his front, holding her upright. She would be wobbly after all that exercise if he let her go. "You've been running for too long, CB. It's time to stop."

She hmphed, slumping against him. "I was in the zone."

"That may be, but you're going to be too sore to get out of bed tomorrow after that workout." He kissed her salty neck, not caring that she was getting him all sweaty. He loved holding her no matter what state she was in.

Magnus came toward them, holding out her water bottle.

Hawking took it, flipped the top open, and held the straw to her lips. "Drink, Little girl."

She frowned, but as soon as she took the first sip, she snagged it from him and drained it. "Guess I was thirsty."

"I should say." He chuckled as he turned her to face him, keeping his hands on her hips to steady her. "I thought it was just your work that held your focus so hard that you shut out the world around you. But it's everything you do, isn't it, Cuddle Bug? You're intense whether you're working, jogging, or even organizing your playroom."

She shrugged.

"Hey," Magnus said from across the room. "I think there's an incoming email." He was leaning over the computer Celeste had been working at.

Celeste shoved the water bottle at Hawking and rushed across the room, though Hawking wasn't at all sure where she got the energy. She'd been about to collapse two seconds ago. Adrenaline had to be pumping through her.

Hurrying to join them, Hawking set the water bottle down and leaned over his Little girl's shoulder to read with her.

She muttered all the words in the email out loud as her head moved back and forth with each line of text. "Wow. I think they believe me." She glanced over her shoulder at Hawking. "They want to interview me. Live. On television." She fidgeted her fingers together, looking pale.

"That's excellent, Cuddle Bug. It's exactly what you were hoping for." He cupped the back of her head and furrowed his brow.

She swallowed. "I know. It's perfect, but it's scary. I'm a scientist, not a television personality." Suddenly, her eyes went wide, and she gasped, went to her knees, and reached up to pat her hair with both hands.

"What's wrong?" He was in a spiral of confusion.

"I can't even do my own hair and makeup," she shouted before groaning. "The only time I've worn any in the past several years was for that gala. You saw the pictures."

"Little girl, no one cares about your hair and makeup. You're stunning without any additions anyway."

She shook her head. "You're just saying that because you're my Daddy, and you have to."

He squatted in front of her and met her eye to eye. "I'm not just saying that, CB. You're a beautiful woman. But I'm sure we can find someone to help you if it will give you more confidence."

"Do you think so?"

"I know so." He'd make some calls and find someone. His biggest concern was keeping her safe. Leaving the safety of Danger Bluff Mountain Resort was risky. Here, he and his team could protect anyone. Once they left the resort and headed into the city, she would be exposed.

Magnus was leaning over on her other side, reading the email closely. "This is in two days. At least they're located on the South Island. It's not too far."

Celeste stood and started pacing while muttering to herself. "You can do this. You *have* to do this. For science. For humanity. Because it's not right to let Dr. Hughes steal your research."

"That's right, CB. That man has obviously pulled this stunt several times. Someone needs to stop him." Hawking was already so proud of his girl. He knew she didn't like the idea of speaking in front of the world, but she would do it.

The elevator opened, and the rest of the team streamed

into the basement—Kestrel, Phoenix, Caesar, and Rocco, plus Sadie.

Sadie rushed over to Celeste. "Did you hear from the reporter?"

"Yes." Celeste pointed at the computer. "He wants to interview me. Live. In two days."

Sadie's face lit up. "That's great." Then her expression fell. "Is it? You don't look too happy."

Celeste stood taller, took a deep breath, and pasted on a smile. "It's great. It's exactly what I need to do."

Sadie rubbed her back. "It's scary, though."

Celeste nodded.

Sadie grinned. "I think we need to do something fun tonight to take your mind off all of this. Dinner will be here in about thirty minutes."

"I got all the supplies for rock painting if everyone is interested," Kestrel suggested.

"That's a great idea," Sadie exclaimed.

Hawking watched his Little girl carefully. If she didn't want to paint rocks tonight, he would shut this idea down. Hell, even though she'd taken a long nap today, she'd also worked out hard. She might like to go to bed early.

Celeste nodded, though. "I think it would be fun." She turned toward Hawking. "Can we do that, Daddy?"

His heart about thudded out of his chest when she deferred to him. "Of course, CB."

She glanced down at herself. She was still sweaty and probably chilled now that her body was cooling down. "Do I have time to shower before dinner?"

Hawking stepped closer, pulled her into his arms, and set his lips on her ear to whisper, "Only if I don't get in with you."

His Little girl gasped and swatted at his chest. "Daddy,"

she whispered. Her cheeks were adorably red, and not just from working out.

He chuckled. “Let’s go get you cleaned up.” He took her hand and led her toward the elevator. “We’ll be back in thirty for dinner and rock painting.”

Chapter Twenty-One

Celeste was distracted as she went through the motions of showering and getting dressed. Truthfully, she barely paid attention. She let her Daddy lead her to their apartment, guide her into the bathroom, and strip her naked.

It wasn't until she stepped under the spray that she came more fully to her senses, but that was short-lived because her Daddy didn't leave her alone to wash. He stripped off his shirt, reached into the shower, and washed her himself.

"Rinse off, Cuddle Bug," he instructed when he was done.

She shuffled under the spray again and let the water run down her body. It felt good on her overused muscles.

When Daddy turned the water off and guided her out of the shower to dry her off with a big fluffy towel, she leaned into him and wrapped her arms around his neck. "Thank you, Daddy. You're the best Daddy in the world."

He lifted her into his arms and carried her into the bedroom, where he sat her on the edge of the bed and tipped her head back. "You're the best Little girl in the world,

Cuddle Bug. I'm sorry for the reasons that brought you to me, but I'm so damn glad I found you. I wondered if I would ever find my Little girl."

When he brought his lips to hers, she wrapped her arms around his neck again, wanting to lose herself in the kiss and forget all the stressful things in her life.

All too soon, he broke free and groaned. "I'd much rather spread you out on this bed and eat you for dinner, but you need nourishment, Little girl. Let's get you dressed and go join the team."

She pushed out her lower lip. "Can we maybe only paint one rock and then come back up here? You could tell everyone I'm exhausted and that you need to put me to bed early."

He chuckled. "It's a deal. Dinner. We'll paint one rock each, and then we'll bail. How's that sound?"

She grinned. "Like a plan."

"Stay right here. I'll grab you something to wear."

She watched his amazing ass as he strode toward the dresser first. He moved to the closet next. When he returned, he held up a purple T-shirt she'd never seen.

She started giggling. "Where did you get that, Daddy?"

"Online. Do you know how many science T-shirts there are?"

She nodded. "I thought I'd seen all of them, but that one is new to me." It had two beakers on the front. One had bubbles coming out of the top. The other had a speech bubble that read, "I think you're overreacting." It was silly and adorable.

"Arms up, CB."

She lifted her arms and let her Daddy pull the shirt over her head. He hadn't given her a bra. She thought about saying something but decided against it. No one would notice in the loose T-shirt, and she didn't feel like putting one on just to go to dinner.

He lifted her to set her on her feet and helped her into panties and a pair of black leggings. Finally, he slid a pair of flip-flops onto her feet.

After a quick trip to the bathroom, where he combed her hair and put it in two low pigtails, he leaned over and kissed her neck. "Ready?"

She was about to tell him to forget dinner and take her to bed when her stomach growled. He was right. She was hungry.

Hawking held her hand as they headed back to the basement. When they arrived, everyone was already gathering around the big table, and the smell coming from the steaming platters in the center made her mouth water.

Celeste shuffled closer. "Are those meat pies?" She inhaled deeply.

Sadie nodded. "Yes. Don't they look delicious? I kept hearing about meat pies from the guests, so I asked the chef if he would make us some. He seemed excited to prepare a locally famous dish for us."

"I love meat pies. I haven't had one in ages. My mother used to make them. They are the perfect comfort food," Celeste informed them as her Daddy pulled out a chair, helped her sit, and pushed her closer to the table.

"I'm sure we're in for a treat," Magnus stated. "So far, everything we've eaten here has been divine. I'm going to have to start working out an extra few hours a week if I don't want to gain twenty pounds."

Celeste giggled. "I don't think any of you are in danger of getting flabby." These six men were the most muscular male specimens she'd ever been this close to. "Do you guys even have an ounce of body fat?"

Kestrel tugged on his ear lobe. "Here, I think."

Rocco snorted. "Delicious dinners or not, if we're going to continue to find and protect a gaggle of Little girls, we're going to need to be fit and sharp."

Phoenix reached for the serving tongs next to the closest platter. "I'm starving. While we eat, we should probably discuss a protection detail for this upcoming trip to town. I'm glad we don't have to leave the south island for Celeste's interview, but I still think we need to be diligent."

Kestrel nodded agreement as he picked up another serving utensil and snagged three pies from the closest platter. "I was thinking about that. What if we transport Celeste by helicopter?"

Caesar took the tongs from Phoenix. "I had similar thoughts. I was thinking if we left the resort by boat, perhaps no one would notice. I bet every entrance and exit available by car is being monitored."

Celeste felt an overwhelming sense of belonging while she listened to these men discuss her safety so matter-of-factly, as if they were a family and she was an important member. It made her tear up a little.

"You okay, CB?" Hawking asked, tipping her chin back to meet her gaze.

She nodded and grabbed her napkin to dab at her eyes. "I don't think I've ever had anyone so devoted to me before, and now, I have all of you."

"Do you have family, Little one?" Rocco asked.

She shook her head as Hawking released her to put a pie on her plate. "My parents were older. They've both passed. I don't have any siblings." She wiped another tear.

Hawking set her plate down and leaned closer to kiss her temple. "You have a family now, Cuddle Bug. All of us." His voice was husky with emotion.

"Thank you. All of you." She looked around the table at everyone's smiling faces and nods of agreement before she sucked back her sadness and turned her attention to the disappearing pies.

The pile of pies was high. Celeste couldn't imagine how the eight of them could possibly eat that much food, but somehow, after dining with this group several times, she figured there wouldn't be a crumb left in about half an hour.

The room grew silent as everyone started eating. In a moment, moans of approval filled the room. "This is so good," Celeste said as she lifted the flakey mince-meat-filled pastry to her lips again.

Rocco groaned. "Delicious. Mine is chicken, I think."

"Mine is steak and mushroom and, maybe, also cheese," Hawking said, tipping it to examine it closer.

"Probably. That's a pretty popular one," Celeste informed him. She eyed his pie longingly.

Hawking caught her, took one more bite, and then snatched hers from her hand and replaced it, trading with her.

When her eyes widened, he grinned and took a huge bite of the mincemeat. "Damn, this one is also fantastic."

Celeste had to fight the tears that wanted to well up again at his kind gesture. He really was the best Daddy in the world. She took a bite of her swapped pie and closed her eyes around the flavors that burst on her tongue.

Sure enough, it didn't take long for all the pies to disappear, though she noted the men made sure she and Sadie had as much to eat as they wanted before they continued filling their stomachs until everything was gone.

"Uh, guys," Sadie said, "we still have dessert."

Rocco set his hand on the back of her chair and shook his head. "No way I can eat another bite."

Sadie giggled. "Bet you'll change your mind when you see what pavlova is." She jumped up and headed to the kitchen area, returning moments later with a tray of the most popular dessert in New Zealand.

Everyone turned to Celeste. "What should we expect, CB?" Hawking asked.

"It's basically a meringue base with whipped cream and berries on top. You'll love it." She couldn't keep from smiling as everyone put one of the national pastries on their plates, even the guys who'd insisted they weren't hungry enough to eat dessert devoured the pavlova.

"Rock time," Kestrel declared as everyone stood to clean up from dinner.

Soon, the table was cleared, and Kestrel had spread out a protective cloth before handing everyone a paper plate to work on and scattering the table with dozens of paints in little bottles. Rocks and brushes were distributed next.

Celeste knew this entire setup was meant to distract her and keep her from worrying about the interview in two days. While they painted, they took turns asking her about her work and what she thought would happen in the future.

An hour later, Celeste held up her finished rock for Daddy to see.

"An orange cat. I love it." He showed her his. He'd covered it in several colors, making it look like a psychedelic swirl.

"That's so pretty, Daddy," she praised.

They gently set their rocks on a clean plate to dry, and then Celeste turned her head to look at him, hoping he would suggest she needed to go to bed now. She even yawned dramatically.

Hawking leaned over and kissed her. "Time for this Little

girl to get some sleep. She's had a very long day." He rose and helped her from her seat. "We'll see you all in the morning."

Everyone waved and said their goodnights as Hawking ushered Celeste toward the elevator.

As soon as it closed, she giggled and covered her mouth. "Do you think they bought my sleepy act?"

"Not a chance, Cuddle Bug." He pulled her into his arms. "It's only seven-thirty. But they won't say anything."

She grinned up at him, too excited about being alone with her Daddy to care if anyone guessed what they might be up to instead of sleeping.

Chapter Twenty-Two

The moment Hawking had his Little girl alone in their apartment, he shut and locked the door before pressing her against it, drawing her arms over her head, and holding her against the wood while he brought his lips to hers.

Her breath hitched when he threaded their fingers together and stretched her arms higher. He loved the little gasps that escaped her mouth against his.

Hawking kissed her senseless until she was panting and whimpering. Finally, he released her lips to nibble a path toward her ear. "I think my Little girl enjoys a bit of restraint."

She rose onto her toes and arched her chest against his without responding.

He nicked her ear with his teeth. "Yeah. She definitely does. What are we going to do about it?" He asked rhetorically while a plan formulated in his mind.

She made a cute little mewling sound.

He pulled back enough to see her face. "Should I tie you to our bed and make you come until you pass out, sated?"

Her eyes widened, but she licked her lips. "I don't know, Daddy. That sounds kind of kinky."

He chuckled. "Age play is pretty kinky, too, Cuddle Bug." He lifted a brow.

She shrugged, at least as much as she could, with him still holding her arms high above her head. "I guess. I don't know much about BDSM, though. Are you going to flog me or something?"

He shook his head. "No, Little girl. I don't think that's likely to be one of our kinks. I was thinking more along the lines of restraining you, blindfolding you, and then sensuously tormenting your sexy body while you writhe and beg me for release."

She shuddered delightfully.

When he pressed his torso more fully against hers and gripped her hands tighter, she sucked in a breath. Yeah, she was interested.

"You won't hurt me, right?"

"Never. I'll spank you when you're naughty because I know you need the release, but that's the only significant impact play I'll ever subject you to, at least without discussing some other implements first. If, down the road you decide you'd like to try floggers, we can discuss it. Tonight, I'm only interested in sensual play."

She licked her lips. "The word I honed in on was 'significant.'"

He chuckled. "I don't think you'll have any complaints if I tap your nipples or your clit when I'm teasing you."

She hesitated a few moments before nodding. "Okay, Daddy," she murmured, putting her trust in him. She had no idea how that made him feel, having his Little girl submit to him with every faith he would treat her like a princess.

He released her hands and swooped down to lift her hips. "Put your legs around me, Little girl."

She wrapped her legs around his back and held on to his neck. She was smiling. A good sign. She was intrigued. It was normal for her to feel skeptical, but he wanted her to have a new sensual experience, and he knew bondage would help her forget her problems. Hopefully, he could make her come so hard that she would sleep like a baby. Lord knew she would need all the rest she could get in the coming days.

When he reached the bed, he lowered her to her feet before peeling the shirt over her head, exposing her fantastic breasts to his view.

As he bent down to draw her leggings and panties off her body, he prayed he could keep from coming prematurely while they played. He was already so turned on by her whimpers and mewls. Now that he had her naked, his cock was at full attention.

"Climb up onto the bed, Cuddle Bug. Lie on your back in the middle and extend your arms and legs toward the corners."

She did as she was told, already panting as he left her to head for the closet. He hadn't brought any kind of official restraints with him to New Zealand, so he would have to improvise.

After a few moments of thought, he decided the best thing would be socks, the longer white kind he wore under boots. He spun around, headed for the dresser, opened the drawer, and grabbed three pairs.

"Socks?" She giggled when he held them up.

"Best form of restraint. They won't cut into your wrists or ankles and won't leave any kind of marks."

"That's good. I'd hate for any of my new friends to wonder why I had handcuff marks on my wrists."

He tied the first two socks together, enjoying the quizzical look on her face. "This pair is going to make the perfect blindfold."

She bit into her bottom lip, but she was breathing heavily, and he loved the way her nipples puckered.

When he climbed onto the bed, he leaned over her and held her gaze. "If you get scared or find out you don't like having your eyes covered or your limbs restrained, just tell Daddy, and I'll stop."

"Okay." Considering the way she squirmed every time he mentioned what he was about to do, he seriously doubted she was going to be disappointed in this scene.

He considered reiterating his words and making sure she understood she had every right to stop him and he would never be disappointed, but he realized he could read his Little girl well enough to know if she was in distress.

"Lift your head, Cuddle Bug." He situated the sock combination so that one of them covered her eyes and one of them rested behind her head, with the knots on both sides. "There. How's that?"

"Weird."

He chuckled and kissed her. "I think you're going to like this. The blindfold will cause your other senses to heighten. Plus, every touch feels more intense when you have no idea where I might stroke your sweet skin next."

Her lips parted as she took shallow breaths.

He slid off the bed and went to work, gently tying her wrists and ankles to the headboard and footboard. When he was done, he let her squirm for a few minutes while he removed all of his clothes except for his boxers.

Nothing was going to contain his cock, but at least this way, it wouldn't bob in front of them until he was ready to fully release it. He snagged two condoms from the drawer and set them on the bed.

After a quick glance around, he decided he needed some toys. More improvisation. He headed for the kitchen, where he grabbed a wooden spoon and then thought a metal spoon might also be nice.

He wouldn't strike her with the spoon in any way that would sting. Small taps could go a long way toward making a person's arousal shoot through the roof.

When he returned, he found her turning her head back and forth. "Daddy?"

"I'm right here, CB." He climbed over her, straddling her waist.

She whimpered.

He set his spoons on the mattress and planted his hands on both sides of her head. Lowering his face until it was inches from hers, he said, "You're already aroused, and I haven't even touched you yet."

She licked her lips.

"I bet you'd like me to kiss you, huh?"

"Yes, please."

"Mmm. Not yet. First, I'm going to tease these pretty little nipples until you're writhing."

The precious buds puckered further at his promise.

Hawking grabbed the metal spoon, flipped it around, and used the handle to circle one of her nipples.

"Oh!" It was good that he was straddling her because she might have flown off the bed if he hadn't been.

He circled the other nipple a few seconds later, getting nearly the same response.

"What is that, Daddy?"

"Mmm. Part of the fun is not knowing."

"It's cold like ice but not wet."

"Mmm-hmm." He flipped the spoon around and flattened the inside of the oval over her swollen bud.

She arched her chest and tugged on her wrists instinctively. "Daddy..."

He removed the spoon and danced the tip down her cleavage and back up to circle her full breasts with the metal edge. Goosebumps rose all over her chest, and she was panting as if she were still on that treadmill.

When he flattened the curved center of the spoon against her other nipple, he asked, "Have you figured out what it is, Cuddle Bug?"

"I think it's a spoon." Her breaths were fast, her chest rising and falling.

"I bet you'll scream when I stroke this cool metal through the folds of your pussy, won't you, Little girl?"

She swallowed hard, but her lips fell open so she could draw in more oxygen.

Hawking flipped the spoon over and lightly tapped one of her nipples.

"Daddy!"

"That's the sweetest sound in the world, Celeste. All it does is make my cock harder. Stay still, Little girl. You're squirming all over the place."

She couldn't get very far between the restraints and him straddling her, but she was wiggling around enough to make it difficult to tease her tight buds. He kept missing when he tried to circle them again.

Without warning, he switched to the wooden spoon and tapped her nipple with the wider base, not hard enough to do anything other than startle her. He'd promised he wouldn't strike her with any force, and he'd meant it.

He didn't give her anymore with the wooden spoon right

away. He didn't want to give away what it had been. Instead, he set it aside, scooted down her body a few inches, and cupped her breasts.

"Awww. I had no idea my breasts were so sensitive," she whispered. "They feel heavy and tight, and my nipples are begging for attention."

He loved the way she was able to voice her feelings and her needs. His ordinarily shy Little girl was growing less inhibited in their bed.

Hawking watched her face as he pinched her nipples between his thumbs and pointers.

"Oh my God," she shouted. "I..."

He smiled. "You like it, don't you?"

"I want more. I want you inside me."

"You'll get more when I'm done playing, Little girl," he said, his tone firm. "First, I want to watch you pant and writhe a bit longer."

She moaned as he pulled on her tight little buds and then twisted them gently.

Finally, he released her nipples and lifted his knees one at a time to move down between her thighs. When he set his palms on her legs and smoothed them up and down from her knees to her pussy without touching her where she needed it most, she bucked her hips off the bed.

He grabbed the metal spoon again and used one hand to hold her torso down while he dragged the cold metal along the outer edges of her pussy lips.

Celeste tried to wiggle, but he was too strong. "Please..."

He flattened the back of the spoon over her clit next, loving the way she cried out as if he'd sucked it into his mouth and flicked it repeatedly with his tongue.

When he drew the handle gently between her lips,

opening her folds to show him how wet she was, she made the cutest sexy sound he'd ever heard.

"Okay, okay. You were right. I'm so horny I'm going to die if you don't fuck me. Please, Daddy."

"Tsk tsk. Such a naughty word from such a pretty mouth."

"Daddy..." Her voice was more of a plea now.

Hawking wanted to do one more thing before he let her come. He swapped the metal spoon for the wooden one again and tapped her clit with the back of the curve.

A long moan filled the room. He knew she was close to orgasm, so he tossed the spoon aside, flattened between her legs, and sucked her pussy into his mouth.

He had to grip both her thighs to hold her steady so he could ravish her with his tongue and his lips. She was squirming so badly it was more like wrangling a bucking bronco.

In seconds, she screamed out her release as her pussy pulsed against his lips.

Hawking continued to lick her through the waves, but as soon as she shuddered, he rose, shrugged off his boxers, and rolled on a condom at warp speed.

And then he was over her, shoving the improvised blindfold off her face so he could look into her eyes as he thrust into her.

She gave him the sexiest moan.

He thrust again, holding her gaze, though he wasn't sure she could fully see him. Her eyes were glazed over with lust.

"I wanna touch you," she pouted.

"Not this time, CB." If he let her get her hands on his shoulders, back, or biceps, he would come in an instant. He loved the way she dug her fingertips into his muscles too much.

She moaned again at his denial and tipped her head back. "I'm on fire, Hawking."

He slid almost out and thrust back in. Usually, he preferred that she call him Daddy, but in the heat of the moment like this, his name sounded golden.

He held himself deep inside her, partly to torment her and partly to keep from coming too soon. After kissing a path to her ear, he whispered, "Next time, I'll flip you over and tie you down on your tummy, Little girl. I bet you'll lose your mind if I take you from behind with your breasts pressing against the bed."

She shivered, and another sweet whimper escaped.

Sweet Jesus, she was so fucking perfect for him.

He couldn't stand waiting another moment, so he eased a hand down between them to find her clit and rubbed the engorged nub while he thrust in and out of her again.

"*Daddy*," she shouted as her pussy gripped his cock harder than ever.

That was all it took. Hawking came harder than ever, too. The only thing that would have made this moment even more intense would have been if he hadn't been wearing protection.

As soon as the threat against her life was over, he would talk to her about birth control. Of course, he wouldn't insist she be the one to protect them against pregnancy if she didn't want to, but a discussion needed to be had.

Celeste didn't even tug on her arms or legs. She lay panting and sated, grinning, her body nearly a liquid.

He didn't pull out. He wanted to stay in her longer, watching her expressions. Her smile and heavy breathing kept his dick hard.

"You were right, Daddy," she finally whispered.

"Daddies are often right, Little girl." He cupped her face

with one hand and stroked a damp lock of hair from her cheek.

Now, he just had to hope he was also right about whatever protection detail they decided upon to keep her safe when they left Danger Bluff. He wasn't going to rest easy until they were back home after her interview.

Chapter Twenty-Three

Two days later...

All six men stood around Celeste with furrowed brows and serious expressions.

Nerves ate at her, making her fidget. She was wearing a new navy pantsuit, a white blouse, and low pumps. Sadie had helped her with her hair and makeup. She felt professional. That was the easy part.

"Let's run through the plan again," Magnus said. "I'll be here in the control room the entire time. Kestrel will be on standby at the helicopter pad in case we need him. Caesar will take you and Hawking by boat to another dock, where Phoenix will pick you both up in the SUV."

Rocco spoke next. "I'll be halfway up the mountain at the main entrance, where I can see nearly every car coming and going from the resort. I'll let Magnus know if I see anyone suspicious on foot or any cars loitering on the surrounding roads."

"And what if you do?" Hawking asked. "We're out of men."

Kestrel nodded. "If necessary, I'll confront them, but as long as people are simply watching the gate, we won't approach them. The more people Dr. Hughes has hanging around Danger Bluff, the fewer people he has available to follow Hawking and Celeste. It will also be an indicator that he has no idea Celeste has left the property."

Celeste tried to listen to every word. They made it sound so simple, but she knew it was anything but simple. Dr. Hughes would want to do anything in his power to stop her from speaking to the world today.

If the scientific community believed her story, Dr. Hughes would be toast. In the last two days, Celeste had been in contact with six other world-renowned scientists who'd had their research stolen by Dr. Hughes.

So far, none of them had felt like they could go up against Dr. Hughes and win. They hadn't had the amount of proof Celeste had to support their accusations. Dr. Hughes was damn good at manipulating people to suck them dry of their expertise and knowledge before turning the tables on them and cutting them loose.

Celeste still wasn't sure if Dr. Hughes had taken a bribe from a pharmaceutical company to keep her research from reaching the public or if he'd simply been greedy and wanted all the credit for her discoveries himself.

"That's a lot to remember," Celeste murmured.

Hawking set a hand on her lower back. "You don't have to remember a thing, Cuddle Bug. I've got it covered."

She turned to him and smiled. It was impossible not to smile every time she looked at him this morning. If she'd thought he looked good in jeans, khakis, and polo shirts, he looked drool-worthy in a suit. And he was wearing a suit—

navy like hers with a white shirt and navy tie. Brown leather shoes completed his outfit.

"Ready?" he asked.

She gave a definitive nod. It wasn't as if she had any options. There was no way she was going to let Dr. Hughes win this time. She had plenty of evidence against him. It was the principle of the matter. He'd done this sort of thing many times. If she didn't confront him and take him down, he would do this again to yet another scientist within months.

Hawking took her hand, gave it a reassuring squeeze, and led her out of the main building and toward the dock, following Caesar.

She was grateful she was able to sit behind the windshield of the speedboat to avoid arriving at the next dock with crazy hair. In addition, Caesar drove them slowly enough to prevent the wind from blowing her carefully arranged hair too badly.

A half-hour later, she and Hawking were in the backseat of the SUV with Phoenix behind the wheel.

"Any problems?" Hawking asked as he reached across to buckle Celeste safely in. He wrapped his larger hand around her small one and held it against her thigh.

"Nope. I did spot two vehicles loitering around the entrance as I left. One of them followed me for a few miles, but I stopped at a gas station and filled up. They drove by slowly but returned to their perch when they saw I was alone. Rocco confirmed that a few minutes ago."

"Good."

Celeste focused on breathing as Phoenix drove them to the studio. As far as anyone knew, Dr. Hughes had no knowledge of the upcoming interview. The woman who'd called her yesterday to confirm the time and location had told her there had been no leaks and only those who were directly affiliated with the interview were aware of it.

It took two hours to reach the studio, and even though Hawking had done everything in his power to distract her with questions about her childhood, schooling, and even science the entire time, she was a nervous wreck as she let him help her exit the SUV.

Phoenix stayed with the car as Hawking led her into the building.

She was surprised by the size of the facility and how many people were hurrying around in the lobby. A woman who identified herself as Charlene—the same woman who'd called Celeste yesterday—was waiting for them in the lobby.

After introductions, she led them to the elevator and then through a maze of studios and camera equipment. It looked to Celeste like six or more people could be filming at the same time. However, her own interview was supposed to be live.

"Would you like to use the restroom before I take you to the stage where you'll be interviewed?" Charlene asked.

"Yes. Thank you." Celeste didn't want to take a risk and end up needing to pee during the interview. It would be stressful enough as it was.

"I'll wait right here, CB," Hawking told her, planting himself directly outside the door to the bathroom.

She loved that she knew he was thinking Cuddle Bug in his mind, but Charlene would have to assume CB was short for Celeste Blanke.

After using the toilet, Celeste headed for the sinks and stopped dead in her tracks. Another woman was in the restroom. Celeste hadn't heard her come in.

The woman wasn't simply a random person needing to pee, either. She was leaning against the center sink, arms crossed, her gaze narrowed on Celeste.

"If you want your boyfriend to stay alive, you'll call off the interview."

Celeste gasped, eyes going wide. "Pardon me?"

"You heard me. Call off the interview. Tell them you lied and have had an attack of conscience. Or tell them you're sick. Do whatever it takes."

"I can't do that," Celeste murmured. "Everyone already knows about my research. It wouldn't even make a difference."

"No one's doubting the research is valid, you idiot." The woman scowled.

Celeste stood frozen. So, this was all about Hughes. He intended to steal the research. It was possible no pharmaceutical company was even aware of the threat to their precious cancer drugs.

"Make the right choice, stupid girl. It would be a shame if anything happened to that hunk of man standing guard outside the bathroom." At that, the woman shoved off the counter and waltzed out the door.

Celeste remained rooted to her spot in the middle of the room. What should she do? Making sure she got credit for a scientific discovery wasn't worth getting Hawking killed.

Suddenly, the door opened and yanked her out of her trance.

"Celeste?"

Her breath hitched when Hawking walked in.

"What are you doing?"

Celeste shuffled toward the sink and turned on the water before pumping soap into her palm and washing her hands. "Just finishing up," she muttered.

He came behind her and set his palms on her shoulders. "You've been in here far longer than necessary. I saw that woman enter and leave the bathroom. Did she say something to you?"

Celeste swallowed. She was a terrible liar, but how was she going to get out of this interview? If she told Hawking the truth, he would tell her not to worry about him. That wasn't acceptable. If anything happened to him, it would be all her fault.

Hawking reached out to turn off the water before pulling a few paper towels from the dispenser and drying her hands from behind. Finally, he spun her around. "Don't lie to me, CB. What happened?"

She set her forehead against his chest and held on to his waist. *Lie. Tell him nothing happened. Tell him you've changed your mind and don't want to do the interview. Tell him it's too stressful, and you don't care who takes credit for your work.*

"Celeste..." There was a warning in his voice. A moment later, he spoke again. "Do you need me to spank you right here in the public restroom before the interview? I will if that's what you need. I'll lock the door, lean you against the wall, pull those pants and panties down to your knees, and spank your bottom. Would you like that?"

She shuddered. Under other circumstances, she might find that scene intriguing. She'd learned two things about spankings. They did indeed help her shed whatever was stressing her out, and they made her horny at the same time.

The problem was Celeste only liked to be spanked because she asked for it—either directly with those precise words or indirectly by intentionally misbehaving. Her infractions in the future would include things like sneaking gummy bears into her pocket or playing in her playroom when she was supposed to be napping.

She'd never be able to lie about something this big.

Tears welled up. She didn't want to cry. Sadie had used waterproof mascara on her, but Celeste didn't want to take any chances of it running down her face.

Lifting her head, she told the truth. "She threatened your life if I go through with the interview."

Hawking drew in a deep breath. "I should've told that bitch to use another restroom. I'm sorry, Little girl. That must've been scary. Thank you for telling me."

"I'll just tell them I don't feel well or something," Celeste rushed to add.

Hawking shook his head. "You'll do no such thing."

"But, Daddy, I wouldn't be able to live with myself if anything happened to you. It would be all my fault." Her voice was shrill.

"Nothing is going to happen to me, Cuddle Bug. If that woman thinks her idle threats will stop you from exposing Dr. Hughes's crimes to the universe, she's sadly mistaken."

"But—"

Hawking shook his head, cutting her off. "But nothing. We're going to head to the studio so you can get the lay of the land, and I'll deal with the woman. I saw her perfectly well. I'll have security pull her up on the camera. This building is filled with cameras."

"That's not going to keep you from getting killed. I'm sure someone paid her to threaten me. She probably doesn't even know anything else. It will be just like the woman who brought me towels at Danger Bluff."

He grabbed her biceps. "Look at me, Celeste." His voice was serious.

She lifted her gaze.

"You're doing the interview, CB. You're doing it not just for yourself but for everyone Hughes has defamed in the past and will steal from in the future. You're doing it because you deserve credit for your discovery. You're doing it because it's the right thing to do. Do not worry about me, Little girl. I'll deal with the woman."

She nodded. "Okay, Daddy."

"That's my girl."

Chapter Twenty-Four

Feeling a dreadful foreboding, Celeste tried to remember to breathe as Charlene led them to the studio where the interview would take place.

The room was crowded with cameramen and technicians, but what made Celeste hesitate was the group of men standing on what was obviously the interview stage. They were dressed in suits and ties. None of them looked like the picture she'd seen of Ben Harbin—the reporter who'd asked her to come this morning.

They all turned to look at her and smiled.

"Dr. Celeste Blanke," an older gentleman said as he stepped forward and held out a hand. "An honor to meet you. I'm Edgar Telafette."

Celeste gasped as she shook his hand. "What are you...?" She didn't even know what to ask.

He grinned. "I gathered everyone I could find. We're here to support you." He took a step back and turned toward the others.

Celeste stood dumbfounded while the other five men introduced themselves. Every scientist she'd contacted in the last few days was here. Tears came to her eyes once more.

"We're going to join you, Dr. Blanke," Dr. Telafette informed her. "No one should face this interview on their own."

She was so incredibly grateful she nearly collapsed.

"Ah, I see you've all met." The new voice came from behind, and Celeste spun to see the reporter from the pictures approaching them.

He held out a hand to her next. "Ben Harbin. Good surprise?" he asked, gesturing to the group of scientists.

"Yes. Thank you." A tremendous relief washed over her. She wouldn't be facing this alone. When she turned to make sure Hawking was still next to her, she breathed a sigh of relief. He was right behind her. He set a hand on her lower back as he quietly introduced himself to the crowd as her boyfriend.

"Everyone needs to take their seats," Charlene announced. She hurried around, pointing to indicate where each person should sit. She positioned Celeste in the chair directly next to Ben Harbin.

When Hawking backed away from the stage, she felt a bit of panic well up inside her. What if that woman hadn't been bluffing? What if someone killed him right here in the studio in front of her?

Hawking spoke to several people in security who scrambled off in different directions. He also pulled out his phone and typed into it. She figured he was letting Phoenix know of the threat.

She was flustered and in no way emotionally ready for this interview when Charlene announced it would begin in "five, four, three, two..."

"Good morning. I'm Ben Harbin. Joining me this morning are six world-renowned scientists, including Dr. Celeste Blanke. I'm sure many of you have heard that name in the last few days. Dr. Blanke is the scientist who discovered a drug that has proven to dramatically slow down the reproduction of cancer cells in the human body, a breakthrough that is hoped to buy precious time for millions of people all over the globe. Unfortunately, Dr. Blanke is also the center of a huge controversy since her former boss, Dr. Alan Hughes, has been accused of stealing Celeste's data and claiming it as his own."

Celeste sat ramrod straight, her gaze often roaming to Hawking as Harbin continued to present the audience with the facts. How many people were watching? How many people would see snippets of this interview in the coming days and weeks?

When Harbin started asking her and her peers questions, she easily fell into step and answered without hesitation. This was her element. She knew everything there was to know about this subject. And bless these other six men for joining her. They each had amazing stories to tell about how Dr. Hughes also stole their research.

When the interview cut to a commercial, Celeste sought out Hawking, and she breathed easier when she found him smiling at her.

Two makeup artists jumped onto the stage during the short break and dabbed at Harbin's face. No one spoke to her.

All too soon, they were back on air, but Harbin's next words sucked all the oxygen out of the room. "Joining us now is Dr. Alan Hughes, the scientist accused of stealing decades' worth of research."

Harbin stood as Dr. Hughes stepped onto the stage while

someone dressed in black added a chair to the other side of Harbin's.

Celeste's jaw dropped. What the hell? Why would Harbin blindside her like this? All of them.

Telafette stood also. He looked like he might strangle someone, and Celeste wasn't sure if he would start with Harbin or Hughes. Either way, he would have to get in line because one glance at Hawking told Celeste he was also close to joining them on stage.

Dr. Hughes shook hands with Harbin before taking his seat, looking as cool as a cucumber.

His grin made her want to vomit. Her ears were ringing. It was difficult to focus on anything Harbin was saying as Hughes painted a picture of the sloppy scientists who'd worked for him over the years. He insinuated that none of the PhDs on the stage were smart enough to put on a pair of shoes, let alone make any scientific breakthroughs.

Just when Celeste thought she might walk off the stage, Harbin changed his tactic and started asking Hughes very specific questions about her research. Harbin had an amazing grasp of her discovery. He'd done his homework. He was framing Hughes.

Hughes smirked. "I don't think your audience is interested in the nitty-gritty of cell growth. It would bore them to tears."

"Oh, on the contrary, Dr. Hughes, I think my audience is *very* interested in hearing how you came to make your discoveries. The process is fascinating."

Hughes chuckled sardonically. "Well, without my papers in front of me, it would be difficult to discuss specifics." He adjusted himself on the chair and straightened his jacket. His face was pale.

Harbin fired off three more questions that any one of the

true scientists on the panel could answer in their sleep. Hughes could not. But more importantly, it didn't matter if the general public understood a word. What mattered was that every important person in the scientific community around the globe was watching or would see this in the next few days. They would all see Hughes making a fool of himself.

Harbin continued. He even dumbed down his questions, posing easier ones that even a high school student might know. Celeste had never realized Hughes was so inept. He'd always been unapproachable at work. Now, she wondered if the man was even a scientist at all.

When she glanced at Hawking, she found two men holding him back, each grasping one of his arms.

Suddenly, Hughes burst out of his chair, causing it to tip backward and fall off the stage. He rushed forward, grabbed Celeste by the arms, and yanked her out of her seat.

She stopped breathing as he shouted at her, inches separating their faces. "Fucking tell them, you cunt. Tell them how you stole my research and presented it as your own. Tell them right now, or I will haunt you for the rest of your life."

Spittle hit her in the face, making her blink, but she said nothing. In seconds, Hughes was yanked back, causing Celeste to fall backward. Luckily, she stumbled into her seat.

Hawking was on the stage, and he had Hughes face first on the floor, a knee on his back. He jerked Hughes's hands behind him and easily secured the asshole. The man certainly had nothing on Hawking. Celeste doubted he'd ever seen the inside of a gym.

People scrambled all around her. Telafette helped her stand and move out of the way while security personnel swarmed the stage, eventually taking over for Hawking.

Celeste thought she might faint. Her legs didn't want to

hold her up. She couldn't believe this had happened. She'd had no idea Harbin had planned this interview to include anyone besides herself, especially not Hughes.

The six men who'd come to support her today all hovered close. Finally, Harbin joined them. He ran a hand through his hair, brows furrowed. "Are you okay?" he asked, looking at Celeste.

Hawking joined them. Before Celeste could respond, he shouted at Harbin. "What the hell were you thinking? You blindsided everyone with this stunt."

Harbin held up both hands. "Hey, man, I had no idea the fucker would attack Dr. Blanke. I simply wanted to nail him to the wall on live television."

"She could've been seriously injured," Hawking shouted.

Celeste rushed forward, set her hands on his chest, and tipped her head back to look at him. "It wasn't ideal, but it worked," she pointed out before nodding behind him. "Look."

Two police officers had arrived and were handcuffing Dr. Hughes while the idiot continued to shout obscenities and threaten everyone in the vicinity with lawsuits.

"Who are *they*?" Dr. Telafette asked, pointing in the other direction.

Celeste looked to find two other men being cuffed. The two men who'd been holding Hawking back to keep him from helping her on the stage.

"They were with Hughes," Harbin informed them. "His personal security detail."

"Yeah, I don't think that was their job," Hawking said sardonically. "They were hired to keep me out of the way at any cost. Luckily, I spotted them and knew they were up to no good before the interview even started."

He wrapped his arms around Celeste, finally making her feel like she might be able to breathe again. When he kissed the top of her head, she inhaled deeply. Was it over?

Chapter Twenty-Five

"Shit. I'm sorry, man," Magnus said later that evening when they were finally all back in the safety of the basement. "I did a lot of digging into Hughes's past, but I never thought to go so far back to discover he never even got a PhD in anything, let alone science."

Hawking shuddered. He hadn't let Celeste out of his sight even for a minute since she'd been attacked on that stage. He hadn't even stopped touching her.

They were all seated on the giant sectional, but he had her on his lap, both arms around her. Every few seconds, he buried his face in her hair and inhaled to remind himself she was alive and well.

"Don't beat yourself up, Magnus," Celeste responded. "I worked for the man, and I never looked him up either. I'll never make a mistake like that again. I've always known prospective employers would dig deep into my past and accomplishments, but it never occurred to me to do the same to them. It's shocking how many years that man got away with pretending he was someone he wasn't. I'm not sure he even knows what a beaker is now. It never occurred to me how easily a person could apply for a job, claim to have credentials they don't have, and then grow and expand without anyone ever questioning their knowledge."

Hawking rubbed her arm. "Sure didn't seem like he knew much about science. You'd think he would've at least picked up on the basics over time, but he seemed dumber than a rock. As for opening the research lab with no background in the field, that part really isn't illegal. He misrepresented himself by claiming he had a PhD, but there's no law that says he needed it to own the facility."

Sadie sat on her Daddy's lap, too. Hawking figured she'd been reliving her own ordeal in her head today while Celeste faced her demons. She was snuggled as close as she could get. "Did they figure out the identity of the woman who approached you in the bathroom?"

Celeste had filled Sadie in on that scary part as soon as they'd arrived.

Hawking nodded. "Security caught her at the door. She never made it out of the building. As we suspected, she was hired by Hughes to intimidate Celeste. It was his last-ditch effort before going on air. There's no evidence he planned to actually do anyone any harm other than hiring the two goons who tried to keep me from approaching the stage. They were no threat to me."

Celeste wrapped her arms around his neck. "You were stronger than both of them put together, Daddy."

He chuckled and rubbed her back. But she was right. They may have grabbed for him, but he'd elbowed them both and had shaken free in seconds.

"Six people were arrested surveilling the property here," Rocco announced. "I have to say it was rather pleasurable watching all the cuffing going on from my perch up in the mountain."

Sadie sighed. "From here, it was just plain scary, Daddy."

He cupped her face. "I was never in any danger, Cookie. Those guys never even knew I was watching."

Magnus leaned back against the cushions. "The police will be interviewing everyone who worked for Hughes. It'll take weeks. I suspect we'll see several more arrests before it's over, but most of them had nothing to do with Celeste or her research. The majority have already come forward to prove their innocence upfront."

Celeste leaned her head against Hawking's shoulder. "I considered several of the employees my friends, or at least my acquaintances. I hope none of them had anything to do with me being fired. It would hurt my soul."

Hawking could sympathize with her. "I bet they only remained silent about your firing under duress."

"I hope so," she murmured.

After a lull in the conversation, Hawking rose to his feet, cradling Celeste in his arms. "We're both exhausted. Thanks for everything today. I'm beyond grateful for the support of such an amazing team."

"Any time, man," Magnus responded.

"Of course," the rest of them added.

Hawking turned to head for the elevator. He wanted to be alone with his girl. No, he *needed* to be alone with her. He needed to hold her naked in his arms and reassure himself she was still alive.

He carried her to their apartment and into the bedroom in silence, depositing her gently on the bed.

When he rose to pull his shirt off, she sat up straighter. "Daddy, I have a question."

"What is it, Cuddle Bug?"

She looked serious and licked her lips several times before continuing. "Did you have cancer at some point?"

He lifted both brows. "No. What makes you think that?"

She shrugged. "It's just that you seem to know a lot about cancer research, and you said that Kingsley rescued everyone on your team at some point in the past. I wondered if he got you the cancer treatments you needed like he did for that woman's son the other day."

Oh, boy. Hawking needed to come clean with her. She didn't deserve for him to keep secrets from her. He dropped his shirt on the floor and sat on the edge of the bed. "I wasn't the one who had cancer. It was my mother."

Her eyes widened. "Oh. Is she still with us?"

"No. Sadly, she passed. I wish she'd had access to the drug you've invented. It might have bought her more time. But I was grateful for the drugs Kingsley bought her. She lived far longer than the experts predicted because of him."

"I'm so sorry for your loss. I know losing a parent is hard. Watching them die of cancer is brutal."

He took her hand and held her gaze. "There's more to that story, CB. Most of it, I'm not proud of. I was in a very low place, thinking only about doing whatever it would take to keep my mother alive when Kingsley's men found me and saved me from a very dangerous situation I'd gotten myself into. They saved my life, and Kingsley paid for the treatment my mother needed."

She crawled forward and threw her arms around his neck before kissing him all over his face. "I understand, Daddy. People will do almost anything to get the treatment they need for a dying relative. You don't have to explain further. I know you're a good man and the bestest Daddy on earth."

He couldn't even respond through the lump in his throat

as he held her and tried to keep his tears at bay. He didn't deserve her.

"Know what else I know?" Celeste asked.

He shook his head.

"I know you'd do whatever that was all over again if you could go back, and that you'd do the same thing if it were me."

He nodded, gritting his teeth against the emotional overload. "I love you so much, Celeste."

"I love you, too, Daddy."

They sat like that for a long time, holding each other tight.

Finally, Celeste leaned back. There was a sparkle in her eyes. "I think now would be a good time to tie me to the bed on my stomach and take me from behind."

His breath hitched at her suggestion. His cock jumped to attention, too. "Are you sure, Cuddle Bug?"

"Yes. I also think you should spank me after you restrain me. I need you to chase away all the icky parts of the ugliness with Alan Hughes with your hand on my bottom so I can stop thinking about all he did. Then, you need to fuck me into the mattress until I can't think of anything else."

He chuckled. "Do you think you might get a rise out of me and earn a spanking by cussing, Little girl?"

"Maybe?" She bit her lip before she sat back and dragged her shirt over her head.

They'd changed out of their formal clothing before joining the rest of the team and Sadie in the basement. Celeste hadn't put on a bra. Her chest was now bare and tempting him.

He kind of wished he could flatten her to the mattress and kiss her senseless before thrusting into her. But his Little girl was asking for bondage and a spanking. No way he would deny her either one.

"Also..." she began, her cheeks turning pink, "you don't need to use condoms if you don't want to, Daddy. I've been on the pill for years, and I get tested regularly. I figure you do, too."

His cock stiffened painfully at that pronouncement. The errant thought wafted through his mind that he'd lost track of discussing this with her due to all the havoc that had ruled their lives. Pushing any thought of the danger that had jeopardized her from his mind, Hawking vowed not to allow Hughes to affect their lives further.

He rose to his feet to remove his jeans, focusing only on her. He nodded to assure her that he was also clean before double-checking. "You sure, Little girl?"

She nodded. "Definitely. I want to feel you bare inside me."

He chuckled. "I don't think it will be very different for you, Cuddle Bug. On the other hand, I will probably come in three seconds and fly off the planet before falling back to Earth and possibly injuring myself," he teased.

She giggled. "I'll hold you down, Daddy."

He tugged her legs forward, causing her to lie on her back so he could pull her leggings and panties off.

When they were both naked, he opened the drawer on the nightstand and pulled out his most recent purchase. When he held up the soft Velcro cuffs, Celeste started giggling.

It was hard to keep a straight face, but he managed to point at the bed and give an order. "On your tummy, naughty girl. Daddy is going to remind you who's in charge."

They were playing, and based on the way she continued

to giggle as she scrambled into position and spread her arms and legs out, she knew that.

"Good girl." He grabbed her first arm and tethered her wrist to the corner, loving how her breath hitched as she stopped laughing. "Why is Daddy going to spank your naughty bottom, Little girl?" he asked playfully.

"Because I said *fuck*," she responded in a Little voice that was far faker than her usual Little. "Naughty girls who use bad words like fuck get their bottoms spanked until they learn to stop saying fuck."

He couldn't keep from chuckling at the number of times she used the word. He swatted her naughty little bottom before securing her last ankle.

He climbed up to situate himself next to her and rubbed her cute derriere. "Remember, you can always tell Daddy to stop when we're playing like this."

"Yes, Daddy. I remember." She squirmed, rubbing her pussy and her tits against the mattress. He didn't have the heart to reprimand her for either. She was already panting and needy.

Hawking didn't want to waste any time. He was desperate to be inside her, and the thought of doing so bare made his mouth water.

Using one hand at the small of her back to hold her steady, he started spanking her pretty bottom with the other. She didn't even flinch this time. She went straight from zero to moaning. Her legs were stiff, and she lifted her head off the bed to arch several times.

"Daddy..." The word was more of a plea than anything else. They both needed the release he'd promised.

Hawking swatted her bottom several more times until her skin was pink and heated before reaching between her legs and thrusting two fingers into her tight channel.

Celeste cried out his name. "Hawking!"

God, he loved her.

He was shaking as he climbed over her body and lodged his cock between her legs. He kissed her neck and whispered in her ear, "I'm not going to last long, Cuddle Bug, and I want you to come first. Can you do that for Daddy?"

She moaned as he reached under her hip, found her clit, and gave it a pinch. Her response made his heart rate pick up and his cock lurch against her opening.

While she rode the waves of her release, he continued to kiss her neck. "That's my good girl. You're so pretty when you come for Daddy." Unable to wait another moment, he lined up with her entrance and thrust into her.

Hawking's breath caught in his throat at the sensation. Stars filled his vision. He'd never felt the tight grip of a woman around his bare cock before. This was a first. It was also the last woman he ever wanted to be with.

As he drove into her from behind over and over, all he could do was thread his fingers with hers stretched out above their heads and use the grip of his hands to tell her how damn good she felt.

Heaven had nothing on Celeste Blanke.

Chapter Twenty-Six

A week later...

Celeste was walking on clouds as she and her Daddy returned to the basement after the best day ever. Several things had made today perfect.

First thing in the morning, the authorities had finally determined everyone who'd been connected with the threat to her life had been apprehended.

Before lunch, she'd gotten a call from a highly esteemed research facility about half an hour from Danger Bluff. They'd offered her a position in their company. She hadn't even started applying for jobs yet, mostly out of fear some people in the scientific community might not believe her. She hadn't wanted to face that possibility. But this company called her cold, saying they wanted to make her an offer before anyone else snatched her up.

It was bigger than that, though. The facility who'd

contacted her had purchased the lab she'd been working for. They now owned the rights to the very research she'd been conducting. Apparently the amount of damage the facility sustained by employing Hughes for so many years under false pretenses was enough that the owner hadn't felt he could recover, and his best bet was to cut his losses and sell.

Celeste had listened to their verbal offer at length. She'd been too stunned to make a decision on the spot and asked them to give her a few days. They'd sent a formal email after hanging up, and she and Hawking had poured over it during lunch.

She hadn't called them back, but she would. They were offering to let her work remotely as much as she needed. She could stay here at Danger Bluff most of the time, but any time she wanted or needed, she could go to their facility. It wasn't that far. They even offered to deliver whatever equipment she needed to do research from this basement.

Magnus had spent the afternoon taking it upon himself to turn one side of the basement into a science lab, making her jump up and down with glee when she saw it.

All six men were smiling indulgently at her, and Sadie was rushing around her new workspace, pointing out all its many assets.

However, the best part of the day had been the long jog on the beach she'd taken with Daddy. She'd coveted a run on that beach from day one, and today, she'd finally been able to do so without fearing for her life. To top it off, she'd found one of Kestrel's painted rocks on the route. It was a black cat. She wondered how many black cat rocks were positioned around the property.

Hawking was overbearing and protective, of course, so he wouldn't be letting her go out running by herself anytime soon, and he'd already told her in no uncertain terms that any time she wanted to work at the research facility, one of them would drive her and pick her up.

His high-handed ways didn't upset her, though. She found him endearing and knew he loved her too much to let her out of his sight.

Her heart was swelling with love and excitement as they all took their places around the big table and filled their plates with another amazing dinner from the kitchen.

Sadie had taken a call from the front desk about ten minutes before dinner, and she remained standing once they were all seated. She had a goofy grin on her face as she looked around the room before holding up an envelope.

Everyone gasped, but Kestrel, Magnus, Phoenix, and Caesar stiffened more than Rocco and Hawking.

"Who's next?" Hawking asked as he pulled Celeste out of her seat and onto his lap.

Sadie waved the envelope around before finally stopping at Kestrel.

Kestrel drew in a deep breath and took it from her hand.

Celeste leaned forward, winking at Sadie.

Kestrel rolled his eyes. "You Little girls need to control yourselves. Just because I've gotten an assignment doesn't mean I'll be finding my own Little in the near future. It could've been a fluke that Rocco and Hawking met their forever Littles the way they did. Kingsley isn't God. He's just a man devoted to saving lives."

Kestrel's hands were shaking as he opened the envelope to dump out the jump drive and piece of paper they all knew would fall out.

He picked up the paper and read:

Kestrel Galison, your marker has been called into effect. Here is your assignment. Protect Zara Lynch. The encrypted drive contains all the background information I can provide you.

Baldwin Kingsley III

Authors' Note

We hope you're enjoying Danger Bluff! Each of the men you've met in this series will get their own happily ever after. Stay tuned for all six books coming soon!

Danger Bluff:

Rocco
Hawking
Kestrel
Magnus
Phoenix
Caesar

About Becca Jameson

Becca Jameson is a USA Today best-selling author of over 140 books. She is well-known for her Wolf Masters series, her Fight Club series, and her Surrender series. She currently lives in Houston, Texas, with her husband. Two grown kids pop in every once in a while too! She is loving this journey and has dabbled in a variety of genres, including paranormal, sports romance, military, reverse harem, dark romance, suspense, dystopian, and BDSM.

A total night owl, Becca writes late at night, sequestering herself in her office with a glass of red wine and a bar of dark chocolate, her fingers flying across the keyboard as her characters weave their own stories.

During the day--which never starts before ten in the morning!--she can be found walking, running errands, or reading in her favorite hammock chair!

...where Alphas dominate...

Becca's Newsletter Sign-up

Join my Facebook fan group, Becca's Bibliomaniacs, for the most up-to-date information, random excerpts while I work, giveaways, and fun release parties!

Facebook Fan Group:
Becca's Bibliomaniacs

Contact Becca:
www.beccajameson.com
beccajameson4@aol.com

facebook.com/becca.jameson.18
x.com/beccajameson
instagram.com/becca.jameson
bookbub.com/authors/becca-jameson
goodreads.com/beccajameson
amazon.com/author/beccajameson

Also by Becca Jameson

Danger Bluff:

Rocco

Hawking

Kestrel

Magnus

Phoenix

Caesar

Roses and Thorns:

Marigold

Oleander

Jasmine

Tulip

Daffodil

Lily

Bite of Pain Anthology: Gemma's Release

Shadowridge Guardians:

Steele by Pepper North

Kade by Kate Oliver

Atlas by Becca Jameson

Doc by Kate Oliver

Gabriel by Becca Jameson

Talon by Pepper North

Blossom Ridge:

Starting Over

Finding Peace

Building Trust

Feeling Brave

Embracing Joy

Accepting Love

Blossom Ridge Box Set One

Blossom Ridge Box Set Two

The Wanderers:

Sanctuary

Refuge

Harbor

Shelter

Hideout

Haven

The Wanderers Box Set One

The Wanderers Box Set Two

Surrender:

Raising Lucy

Teaching Abby

Leaving Roman

Choosing Kellen

Pleasing Josie

Honoring Hudson

Nurturing Britney

Charming Colton

Convincing Leah

Rewarding Avery

Impressing Brett

Guiding Cassandra

Surrender Box Set One

Surrender Box Set Two

Surrender Box Set Three

Open Skies:

Layover

Redeye

Nonstop

Standby

Takeoff

Jetway

Open Skies Box Set One

Open Skies Box Set Two

Shadow SEALs:

Shadow in the Desert

Shadow in the Darkness

Holt Agency:

Rescued by Becca Jameson

Unchained by KaLyn Cooper

Protected by Becca Jameson

Liberated by KaLyn Cooper

Defended by Becca Jameson

Unrestrained by KaLyn Cooper

Delta Team Three (Special Forces: Operation Alpha):

Destiny's Delta

Canyon Springs:

Caleb's Mate

Hunter's Mate

Corked and Tapped:

Volume One: Friday Night

Volume Two: Company Party

Volume Three: The Holidays

Project DEEP:

Reviving Emily

Reviving Trish

Reviving Dade

Reviving Zeke

Reviving Graham

Reviving Bianca

Reviving Olivia

Project DEEP Box Set One

Project DEEP Box Set Two

SEALs in Paradise:

Hot SEAL, Red Wine

Hot SEAL, Australian Nights

Hot SEAL, Cold Feet

Hot SEAL, April's Fool

Hot SEAL, Brown-Eyed Girl

Dark Falls:

Dark Nightmares

Club Zodiac:

Training Sasha

Obeying Rowen

Collaring Brooke

Mastering Rayne

Trusting Aaron

Claiming London

Sharing Charlotte

Taming Rex

Tempting Elizabeth

Club Zodiac Box Set One

Club Zodiac Box Set Two

Club Zodiac Box Set Three

The Art of Kink:

Pose

Paint

Sculpt

Arcadian Bears:

Grizzly Mountain

Grizzly Beginning

Grizzly Secret

Grizzly Promise

Grizzly Survival

Grizzly Perfection

Arcadian Bears Box Set One

Arcadian Bears Box Set Two

Sleeper SEALs:

Saving Zola

Spring Training:

Catching Zia

Catching Lily

Catching Ava

Spring Training Box Set

The Underground series:

Force

Clinch

Guard

Submit

Thrust

Torque

The Underground Box Set One

The Underground Box Set Two

Wolf Masters series:

Kara's Wolves

Lindsey's Wolves

Jessica's Wolves

Alyssa's Wolves

Tessa's Wolf

Rebecca's Wolves

Melinda's Wolves

Laurie's Wolves

Amanda's Wolves

Sharon's Wolves

Wolf Masters Box Set One

Wolf Masters Box Set Two

Claiming Her series:

The Rules

The Game

The Prize

Claiming Her Box Set

Emergence series:

Bound to be Taken

Bound to be Tamed

Bound to be Tested

Bound to be Tempted

Emergence Box Set

The Fight Club series:

Come

Perv

Need

Hers

Want

Lust

The Fight Club Box Set One

The Fight Club Box Set Two

Wolf Gatherings series:

Tarnished

Dominated

Completed

Redeemed

Abandoned

Betrayed

Wolf Gatherings Box Set One

Wolf Gathering Box Set Two

Durham Wolves series:

Rescue in the Smokies

Fire in the Smokies

Freedom in the Smokies

Durham Wolves Box Set

Stand Alone Books:

Blind with Love

Guarding the Truth

Out of the Smoke

Abducting His Mate

Wolf Trinity

Frostbitten

A Princess for Cale/A Princess for Cain

Severed Dreams

Where Alphas Dominate

About Pepper North

Ever just gone for it? That's what *USA Today* Bestselling Author Pepper North did in 2017 when she posted a book for sale on Amazon without telling anyone. Thanks to her amazing fans, the support of the writing community, Mr. North, and a killer schedule, she has now written more than 80 books!

Enjoy contemporary, paranormal, dark, and erotic romances that are both sweet and steamy? Pepper will convert you into one of her loyal readers. What's coming in the future? A Daddypalooza!

Sign up for Pepper North's newsletter

Like Pepper North on Facebook

Join Pepper's Readers' Group for insider information and giveaways!

Follow Pepper everywhere!
Amazon Author Page
BookBub
FaceBook
GoodReads
Instagram
TikToc
Twitter
YouTube
Visit Pepper's website for a current checklist of books!

amazon.com/author/pepper_north
bookbub.com/profile/pepper-north
facebook.com/AuthorPepperNorth
instagram.com/4peppernorth
pinterest.com/4peppernorth
x.com/@4peppernorth

Also By Pepper North

Don't miss future sweet and steamy Daddy stories by Pepper North? Subscribe to my newsletter!

Shadowridge Guardians

Combining the sizzling talents of bestselling authors Pepper North, Kate Oliver, and Becca Jameson, the Shadowridge Guardians are guaranteed to give you a thrill and leave you dreaming of your own throbbing motorcycle joyride.

Are you daring enough to ride with a club of rough, growly, commanding men? The protective Daddies of the Shadowridge Guardians Motorcycle Club will stop at nothing to ensure the safety and protection of everything that belongs to them: their Littles, their club, and their town. Throw in some sassy, naughty, mischievous women who won't hesitate to serve their fair share of attitude even in the face of looming danger, and this brand new MC Romance series is ready to ignite!

Available on Amazon

Danger Bluff

Welcome to Danger Bluff where a mysterious billionaire brings together a hand-selected team of men at an abandoned resort in New Zealand. They each owe him a marker. And they all have something in common–a dominant shared code to nurture and protect. They will repay their debts one by one, finding love along the way.

Available on Amazon

A Second Chance For Mr. Right

For some, there is a second chance at having Mr. Right. Coulda, Shoulda, Woulda explores a world of connections that can't exist... until they do. Forbidden love abounds when these Daddy Doms refuse to live with regret and claim the women who own their hearts.

Available on Amazon

Little Cakes

Welcome to Little Cakes, the bakery that plays Daddy matchmaker! Little Cakes is a sweet and satisfying series, but dare to taste only if you like delicious Daddies, luscious Littles, and guaranteed happily-ever-afters.

Available on Amazon

Dr. Richards' Littles®

A beloved age play series that features Littles who find their forever Daddies and Mommies. Dr. Richards guides and supports their efforts to keep their Littles happy and healthy.

Available on Amazon

Note: Zoey; Dr. Richards' Littles® 1 is available FREE on Pepper's website:

4PepperNorth.club

SANCTUM

Pepper North introduces you to an age play community that is isolated from the surrounding world. Here Littles can be Little, and Daddies can care for their Littles and keep them protected from the outside world.

Available on Amazon

Soldier Daddies

What private mission are these elite soldiers undertaking? They're all searching for their perfect Little girl.

Available on Amazon

The Keepers

This series from Pepper North is a twist on contemporary age play romances. Here are the stories of humans cared for by specially selected Keepers of an alien race. These are science fiction novels that age play readers will love!

Available on Amazon

The Magic of Twelve

The Magic of Twelve features the stories of twelve women transported on their 22nd birthday to a new life as the droblin (cherished Little one) of a Sorcerer of Bairn. These magic wielders have waited a long time to take complete care of their droblin's needs. They will protect their precious one to their last drop of magic from a growing menace. Each novel is a complete story.

Available on Amazon

Printed in Great Britain
by Amazon